BOOKS

D0313942

Venus Drive
Stories by Sam Lipsyte

"Sam Lipsyte is a wickedly gifted writer. *Venus Drive* is filled with grimly satisfying fractured insights and hardcore humor. But it also displays some inspired sympathy for the daze and confusion of its characters. Above all it's wonderfully written and compulsively readable with brilliant and funny dialogue, a collection that represents the emergence of a very strong talent."
  — Robert Stone

"Sam Lipsyte can get blood out of a stone—rich, red human blood from the stony sterility of contemporary life. His writing is gripping—at least I gripped this book so hard my knuckles turned white."
  —Edmund White

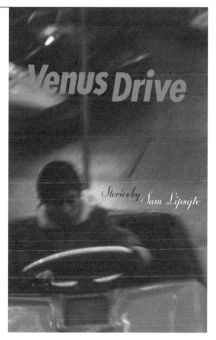

Karoo
A Novel by Steve Tesich

"Fascinating—a real satiric invention full of wise outrage."
  —Arthur Miller

"A powerful and deeply disturbing portrait of a flawed, self-destructive, and compulsively fascinating figure."
  —*Kirkus Reviews* (starred)

"Saul Karoo is a new kind of wild man, the sane maniac. Larger than life and all too human, his out-of-control odyssey through sex, death, and show business is extreme, and so is the pleasure of reading it. Steve Tesich created a fabulously Gargantuan comic character."
  —Michael Herr

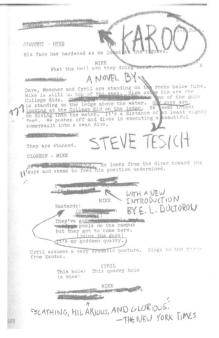

Some Hope
A Trilogy by Edward St. Aubyn

"Tantalizing . . . A memorable tour de force."
  —*The New York Times Book Review*

"Hilarious and harrowing by turns, sophisticated, reflective, and brooding."
  —*The New York Review of Books*

"Feverishly good writing . . . Full of Algonquin wit on the surface while roiling underneath. *Some Hope* is a hell of a brew, as crisp and dry as a good English cider and as worth savoring as any of Waugh's most savage volleys."
  —*The Ruminator Review*

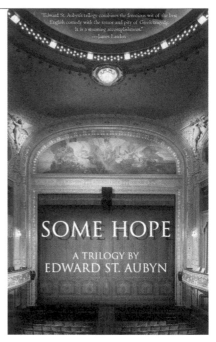

Mother's Milk
A Novel by Edward St. Aubyn

"St. Aubyn's caustic, splendid novel probes the slow violence of blood ties—a superbly realized agenda hinted at in the novel's arresting first sentence: 'Why had they pretended to kill him when he was born?'"
  —*The Village Voice*

"Postpartum depression, assisted suicide, adultery, alcoholism—it's all here in St. Aubyn's keenly observed, perversely funny novel about an illustrious cosmopolitan family and the mercurial matriarch who rules them all."
  —*People*

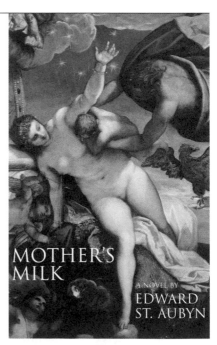

OPEN CITY

Actual Air
Poems by David Berman

"David Berman's poems are beautiful, strange, intelligent, and funny. They are narratives that freeze life in impossible contortions. They take the familiar and make it new, so new the reader is stunned and will not soon forget. I found much to savor on every page of *Actual Air*. It's a book for everyone."
    —James Tate

"This is the voice I have been waiting so long to hear . . . Any reader who tunes in to his snappy, offbeat meditations is in for a steady infusion of surprises and delights."
    —Billy Collins

My Misspent Youth
Essays by Meghan Daum

"An empathic reporter and a provocative autobiographer . . . I finished it in a single afternoon, mesmerized and sputtering."
    —*The Nation*

"Meghan Daum articulates the only secret left in the culture: discreet but powerful fantasies of romance, elegance, and ease that survive in our uncomfortable world of striving. These essays are very smart and very witty and just heartbreaking enough to be deeply pleasurable."
    —Marcelle Clements

OPEN CITY

New York City, Winter 2008–2009
Number Twenty-Six

BOOKS

Goodbye, Goodness
A Novel by Sam Brumbaugh

"*Goodbye, Goodness* is the rock n' roll *Great Gatsby*."
—*New City Chicago*

"Sam Brumbaugh's debut novel couldn't be more timely. *Goodbye, Goodness* boasts just enough sea air and action to make an appealing summer read without coming anywhere near fluffsville."
—*Time Out New York*

"Beautifully captures the wrung-out feel of a depleted American century."
—*Baltimore City Paper*

The First Hurt
Stories by Rachel Sherman

"Sherman's writing is sharp, hard, and honest; there's a fearlessness in her work, an I'm-not-afraid-to-say-this quality. Because she knows that most of us have thought the same but didn't have the guts to say it."
—*Boston Phoenix*

"Rachel Sherman writes stories like splinters: they get under your skin and stay with you long after you've closed the book. These haunting stories are both wonderfully, deeply weird and unsettlingly familiar."
—Judy Budnitz

Long Live a Hunger to Feed Each Other
Poems by Jerome Badanes

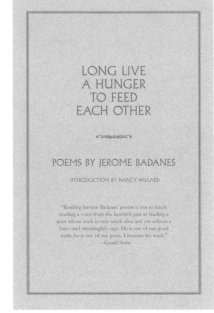

"Reading Jerome Badanes's poems is not so much reading a voice from the heartfelt past as reading a poet whose work is very much alive and yet reflects a lost—and meaningful—age. He is one of our good souls; he is one of our poets. I treasure his work."
  —Gerald Stern

"The best best book publishing story of the year."
  —Poetry

Farewell Navigator
Stories by Leni Zumas

"Zumas gives socially awkward, mysteriously gifted and self-destructive outcasts spellbinding, unflinching voice. . . . It's a powerful, irresistible collection."
  —Publishers Weekly

"Leni Zumas's writing is fearless and swift, sassy and sensational."
  —Joy Williams

"I have never read stories like these before and I can't get them out of my head. Her language is real sorcery—it dismantles the world you think you know and takes you to strange, fecund territories of the imagination. "
  —Karen Russell

BOOKS

Love Without
Stories by Jerry Stahl

"[Stahl]...knows how to shock us into
laughter, and his best work mines the
grotesque for pathos, a tradition that
includes Flannery O'Connor, Barry
Hannah, and Denis Johnson . . .The key
isn't whom he writes about, but at what
depth . . . Stahl plunges us into depraved
worlds with a keen intensity of purpose,
and his addled protagonists run up hard
against the truth of their desires."
— *Los Angeles Times*

"Tender and gut-busting."
— *L.A. Weekly*

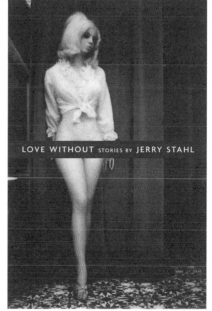

Why the Devil Chose New England for His Work
Stories by Jason Brown

"*Why the Devil Chose New England for
His Work* links gem-cut stories of trou-
bled youths, alcoholics, illicit romances,
the burden of inheritance, and the bane
of class, all set in the dense upper
reaches of Maine, and delivers them
with hope, heart, and quiet humor."
—Lisa Shea, *Elle*

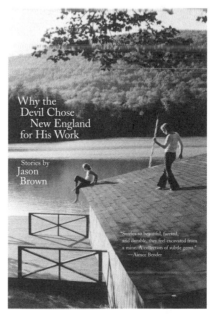

Flight Patterns

A Century of Stories about Flying

Edited by Dorothy Spears

Contributions by

Thomas Beller
John Bowe
Bernard Chabbert
Roald Dahl
Meghan Daum
Joan Didion
Andre Dubus
Amelia Earhart
Mary Gaitskill
Barry Hannah
Joseph Heller
Gary Horn
Erica Jong
Walter Kirn

Charles Lindbergh
Beryl Markham
Alice Munro
Antoine de Saint-Exupéry
James Salter
Saïd Sayrafiezadeh
David Sedaris
Mary Lee Settle
Dorothy Spears
Jerry Stahl
Tom Wolfe
Tobias Wolff
Wilbur & Orville Wright
Linda Yablonsky

Spring 2009

OPEN CITY

RICE

292 ELIZABETH ST

N O H O

212-226-5775

RICENY.COM

Twenty-three years after her startlingly original debut, *The Beans of Egypt, Maine,* Carolyn Chute returns to Egypt with an impassioned and emotive novel that reminds us why she remains the preeminent contemporary voice of America's working poor.

THE SCHOOL ON HEART'S CONTENT ROAD

CAROLYN CHUTE

AUTHOR OF THE BEANS OF EGYPT, MAINE

"[Carolyn Chute] returns with more moxie, righteous indignation, and artistry than ever before to challenge our notions of democracy, family, and fiction . . . [and illuminate] what exactly poverty, injustice, and the corporate imperative do to body and soul."—DONNA SEAMAN, *BOOKLIST* (STARRED REVIEW)

ATLANTIC MONTHLY PRESS an imprint of Grove/Atlantic, Inc.
Distributed by Publishers Group West   www.groveatlantic.com

OPEN CITY

Open City is published by Open City, Inc., a nonprofit corporation. Donations are tax-deductible to the extent allowed by the law. A one-year subscription (3 issues) is $30; a two-year subscription (6 issues) is $55. Make checks payable to: Open City, Inc., 270 Lafayette Street, Suite 1412, New York, NY 10012. For credit-card orders, see our Web site: www.opencity.org. E-mail: editors@opencity.org.

Open City is a member of the Council of Literary Magazines and Presses and is indexed by Humanities International Complete.

Open City gratefully acknowledges the generous support of the family of Robert Bingham. We also thank the New York State Council on the Arts and the Annenberg Foundation. See the page following the masthead for additional donor acknowledgments.

State of the Arts

NYSCA

Front and back covers by Balint Zsako. Front: *Untitled,* collage, 2008. Back: *Untitled,* collage, 2008. Courtesy of the artist and The Proposition Gallery.

Front page photograph by Jocko Weyland.

ISBN-13: 978-1-890447-50-2
ISBN-10: 1-890447-50-1
ISSN: 1089-5523

OPEN CITY

EDITORS
Thomas Beller
Joanna Yas

ART DIRECTOR
Nick Stone

EDITOR-AT-LARGE
Adrian Dannatt

CONTRIBUTING EDITORS
Jonathan Ames
Elizabeth Beller
David Berman
Aimée Bianca
Will Blythe
Jason Brown
Sam Brumbaugh
Patrick Gallagher
Amanda Gersh
Laura Hoffmann
Jan de Jong
Kip Kotzen
Anthony Lacavaro
Alix Lambert
Vanessa Lilly
Sam Lipsyte
Jim Merlis
Honor Moore
Robert Nedelkoff
Parker Posey
Beatrice von Rezzori
Elizabeth Schmidt
Lee Smith
Alexandra Tager
Tony Torn
Jocko Weyland
Edmund White

INTERNS
Joanna Bock
Emily Hunt

READERS
Mike Gardner
Evan Hansen
Michael Hornburg
Sarah LaPolla
Lina Makdisi
Rowland Miller

FOUNDING EDITORS
Thomas Beller
Daniel Pinchbeck

FOUNDING PUBLISHER
Robert Bingham

OPEN CITY WOULD LIKE TO THANK THE FOLLOWING FOR THEIR GENEROUS CONTRIBUTIONS

Patrons ($1,000 or more)
Clara Bingham
Joan Bingham
Belle & Henry Davis
Wendy Flanagan
Laura Fontana & John J. Moore
Laura Hoffman
Alex Kuczynski
Vanessa & John Lilly
Eleanor & Rowland Miller
Scott Smith
Dorothy Spears
Mary & Jeffrey Zients

Donors ($500 or more)
Robert Scott Asen
Hava Beller
David Selig (Rice Restaurant)
Amine Wefali (Zaitzeff Restaurant)

Contributors ($150 or more)

Molly Bingham
Duncan Birmingham
Paula Bomer
Nina Collins
Joe Conason & Elizabeth Wagley
Paula Cooper
Holly Dando
Edward Garmey
David Goodwillie
Pierre Hauser
Carol Irving
Kathy Kemp
Jason Kliot & Joana Vicente

Caitlin Macy & Jeremy Barnum
William Morton
Rulonna Neilson
Tim Nye
Rick Rofihe
Robert Soros &
     Melissa Schiff Soros
Georgia & Terry Stacey
Jennifer Sturman
Judson Traphagan
Elizabeth Wagley & Joe Conason
Shelley Wanger
Chris Young

Friends

Alex Abramovich
Jonathan Ames
Lucy Anderson
Tony Antoniadis
Harold Augenbraum
Noah Baumbach
Madeleine Beckman
Madison Smartt Bell
Elizabeth Beller
Betsy Berne
Aimée Bianca
Andrew Blauner
Ghurron Briscoe
Sam Brumbaugh
Toby Bryce
Jocelyn Casey-Whitman
Simon Constable
Thomas Cregan
Adrian Dannatt
John Donahue
Christopher Edgar
Erin Edmison
Deborah Eisenberg
Lisa Evanchuck
Mary Evans
Jofie Ferrari-Adler
Mike Gardner
Deborah Garrison
Alice Gordon
Melissa Gould
Melissa Grace
Rebecca Green
Will Heinrich
Jessamyn Hope
Gerald Howard
Amy Hundley
Anthony Lacavaro
Deborah Landau

Matt Lee
Guy Lesser
Sam Lipsyte
Stephen Mark
Pearson Marx
Vestal McIntyre
Paul Morris
Carolyn Murnick
Christopher Nicholson
Ethan Nosowsky
Nancy Novogrod
Sylvia Paret
Vince Passaro
Francine Prose
Beatrice von Rezzori
Anne Rivers
Saïd Sayrafiezadeh
Elizabeth Schmidt
Richard Serra
Wallace Shawn
Rachel Sherman
Claudia Silver
Debra Singer
Betsy Smith
Lee Smith
Valerie Steiker
Anna Stein
Ben Stiller
Nick Stone
Robert Stone
Stefanie Syman
Paul Tullis
Ben Turner
Dean Wareham & Britta Phillips
Cecilia & John Weyland
Malerie Willens
Leni Zumas
Todd Zuniga

siglio

Siglio is a new, independent press in Los Angeles publishing uncommon books that live at the intersections and interstices of art and literature.

Siglio books defy easy categorization. They are innovative, hybrid works in which the relationships between image and text are complex and dynamic; in which narrative forms are reinvented, subverted, or redefined; in which seemingly dissimilar things collide or converge in order to yield something surprising, intriguing, and provocative.

We aim to cultivate wider audiences for original, challenging work by renowned as well as unknown, forgotten or marginalized artists and writers; to nurture collaborations and ignite conversations across various boundaries and disciplines; and to (re)issue work long unavailable, untranslated, or originally published in compromised form.

Sign up for the mailing list at **www.sigliopress.com** to receive a **15% discount** (mention Open City!). All Siglio website orders also receive special edition ephemera available nowhere else. You'll get advance notice about new titles, limited editions and ephemera collections, special discounts, and additions to the Siglio library where you'll find on-line interviews, essays, recommended reading, and other resources.

Available Now: The Nancy Book by Joe Brainard

From 1963 to 1978 Joe Brainard created more than 100 works of art that appropriated the classic comic strip character Nancy and sent her into an astonishing variety of spaces, all electrified and complicated by the incongruity of her presence. With 78 full page illustrations, original essays by Ann Lauterbach and Ron Padgett, and collaborations with Bill Berkson, Ted Berrigan, Robert Creeley, Frank O'Hara, James Schuyler, and others. Hardback, 144 pages. $39.50

The Nancy Book Limited Edition is slipcased with a beautiful, hand-pulled lithograph of "Untitled (Nancy with Gun)," housed in a foil-stamped portfolio. Inquire about availability.

Forthcoming Spring 2009: Several Gravities by Keith Waldrop

ANNA
CLOTHES FOR WOMEN

150 East 3rd Street at Avenue A
New York City
212.358.0195
www.annanyc.com

TWO DOCUMENTARIES

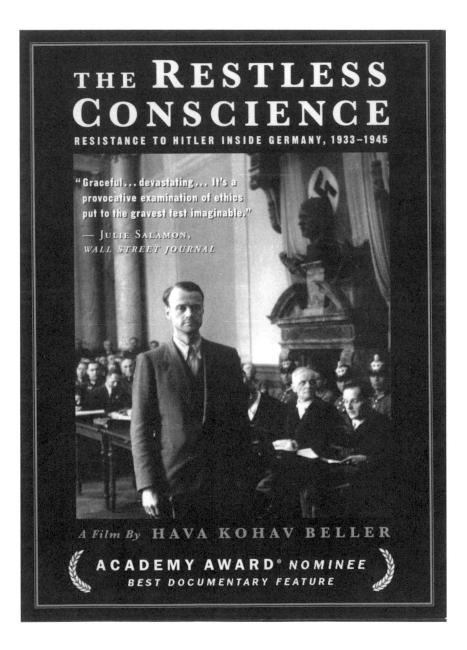

THE **RESTLESS CONSCIENCE**

RESISTANCE TO HITLER INSIDE GERMANY, 1933–1945

"Graceful... devastating... It's a
provocative examination of ethics
put to the gravest test imaginable."
— JULIE SALAMON,
WALL STREET JOURNAL

A Film By HAVA KOHAV BELLER

ACADEMY AWARD® NOMINEE
BEST DOCUMENTARY FEATURE

anderbo.com

fiction   poetry   "fact"   photography

RROFIHE TROPHY!

2008 Winner
Caedra Scott-Flaherty

FOR HER STORY
"Piecemeal"

There were 200 stories submitted to the
2008 RRofihe Trophy Contest.

Caedra Scott-Flaherty's story
is published in this issue.
She also receives $500 and a trophy.

2009 RRofihe Trophy Guidelines

- Stories should be typed, double spaced, on 8 1/2 x 11 paper with the author's name and contact information on the first page and name and story title on the upper right corner of remaining pages
- Submissions must be postmarked by September 15, 2009
- Limit one submission per author
- Author must not have been previously published in *Open City*
- Mail submissions to RRofihe, 270 Lafayette Street, Suite 1412, New York, NY 10012
- Enclose self-addressed stamped business envelope to receive names of winner and honorable mentions
- All manuscripts are non-returnable and will be recycled
- Reading fee is $10. Check or money order payable to RRofihe
- Judged by Rick Rofihe; 2009 Contest Assistant: Carolyn Wilsey

'Writers in New York

June 1–25, 2009

Writers in New York offers poets and fiction writers an opportunity to develop their craft while living the writer's life in Greenwich Village. Students participate in daily workshops and craft classes, are mentored by accomplished professional writers, and attend readings and talks by acclaimed New York-based writers and editors. Students in the program work intensively to generate new writing, study great literary works by other writers, and participate in a lively series of readings, lectures, literary walking tours, and special events.

FACULTY

Matthew Rohrer
Elissa Schappell
Helen Schulman
Brenda Shaughnessy
Irini Spanidou
Darin Strauss

Deborah Landau (*Director*)
Joanna Yas (*Associate Director*)

VISITING WRITERS & EDITORS

Joshua Beckman, Thomas Beller, Jason Brown, Marcelle Clements, Nick Flynn, Keith Gessen, Sam Lipsyte, Rachel Sherman, Rebecca Wolff, Matthew Zapruder, and more

Visit us at www.cwp.as.nyu.edu/page/summer09

LOST AND FOUND

STORIES FROM NEW YORK

EDITED BY THOMAS BELLER

Essays from Mr. Beller's Neighborhood by:

Saïd Sayrafiezadeh, Rachel Sherman, Bryan Charles,
Phillip Lopate, Jonathan Ames, Alicia Erian,
Madison Smartt Bell, Betsy Berne, Thomas Beller,
Sam Lipsyte, and more

Spring 2009
Mr. Beller's Neighborhood Books
Distributed by W.W. Norton

www.mrbellersneighborhood.com

CONTRIBUTORS' NOTES

HENRY ALCALAY has published half a dozen stories in various journals and anthologies. He lives in New York City.

MOHAMMED NASEEHU ALI, a native of Ghana, is a writer and musician. Ali's fiction and essays have been published in *The New Yorker*, *The New York Times*, *Mississippi Review*, *Bomb*, *A Gathering of the Tribes*, and *Essence*. A graduate of Bennington College, he lives in Brooklyn.

PRISCILLA BECKER's first book of poems, *Internal West*, won *The Paris Review* book prize, and was published in 2003. Her second book, *Stories That Listen*, is forthcoming from Four Way Books. Her poems have appeared in *Fence*, *Open City*, *The Paris Review*, *Small Spiral Notebook*, *The Boston Review*, *Raritan*, and *Verse*. She has published music reviews in *The Nation* and *Filter*; book reviews in the *New York Sun*; and essays in *Cabinet* and *Open City*. Her essays have also been anthologized by Soft Skull Press, Anchor Books, and Sarabande. She teaches poetry at Pratt Institute, Columbia University, and in her apartment.

WILLIAM BENTON's most recent book is *Madly*, a novel.

JOHN FANDEL, born in 1925 in Yonkers, has published in *Poetry*, *The New Republic*, *Hudson Review*, *The Catholic Worker*, and *The New Yorker*, where his much-anthologized and taught poem "Indians" first appeared. He has taught at Notre Dame, Fordham, Portsmouth Abbey, and Manhattan College. The Frost Poetry Scholar at Breadloaf, he also won the Reynolds Lyric Award from the Poetry Society of America and was longtime poetry editor of *Commonweal*. He is the author of numerous books, including *Testament*, *The Deserted Greenhouse*, *A Midnight Question*, *The Sea Pacific*, and *Out of Our Blue*.

BENJAMIN GOLLIVER was born in Portland, Oregon. He earned a BA from the Johns Hopkins University Writing Seminars and currently lives in Lake Oswego, Oregon. He writes regularly about his hometown team, the Portland Trail Blazers.

BRAD GOOCH is the author of *City Poet*, the acclaimed biography of Frank O'Hara. The recipient of National Endowment for the Humanities and Guggenheim fellowships, he earned his PhD at Columbia University and is a professor of English at William Paterson University in New Jersey. His book *Flannery: A Life of Flannery O'Connor* is forthcoming in February 2009.

KIRSTY GUNN is the author of five books of fiction and, most recently, a collection of poetry and essays entitled *44 Things*. She is a professor of writing at the University of Dundee and lives in Scotland and London with her husband and two daughters.

CHRISTOPHER KANG is a recent graduate of the Iowa Writers' Workshop. His poetry and fiction have appeared or are forthcoming in *Gulf Coast*, *The Massachusetts Review*, *Cimarron Review*, *jubilat*, *The L Magazine*, and *Columbia*.

JENNIFER KRONOVET is the author of the poetry collection *Awayward*, which is forthcoming from BOA Editions in spring 2009. She is the cofounder and coeditor of *Circumference: The Journal of Poetry in Translation*.

STRAWBERRY SAROYAN is the author of *Girl Walks into a Bar: A Memoir*. She is completing a TV pilot for a drama about escorts in 1970s Hollywood.

ELIZABETH SCHMIDT has been a contributing editor at *Open City* since issue number four. She has edited poems for *The New Yorker* and *The New York Times Book Review*, reviews books for *Vogue* and *The New York Times Book Review*, and teaches American literature at Sarah Lawrence College.

CAEDRA SCOTT-FLAHERTY is from Rochester, New York. A graduate of Brown University, she served as an AmeriCorps member in North Carolina, and is currently an MFA candidate at New York University's creative writing program. She teaches playwriting and visual arts to incarcerated youth, and is a dancer and choreographer. This is her first published story.

CHRIS SPAIN grew up in South America. He is the author of the story collection *Praying for Rain* His stories have appeared in *The Antioch Review*, *Story*, *The Quarterly*, *Story Quarterly*, *Zoetrope*, and the *Pushcart Prize Anthology*.

MATTHEW SPECKTOR's first novel, *That Summertime Sound*, will appear in July 2009 from MTV Books. He lives in Los Angeles.

BALINT ZSAKO was born in Budapest, Hungary, in 1979. He immigrated to Canada in 1989 and currently lives and works in New York City. He is represented by The Proposition Gallery in New York, Katharine Mulherin Gallery in Toronto, and Wilde Gallery in Berlin. His Web site is www.balintzsako.com.

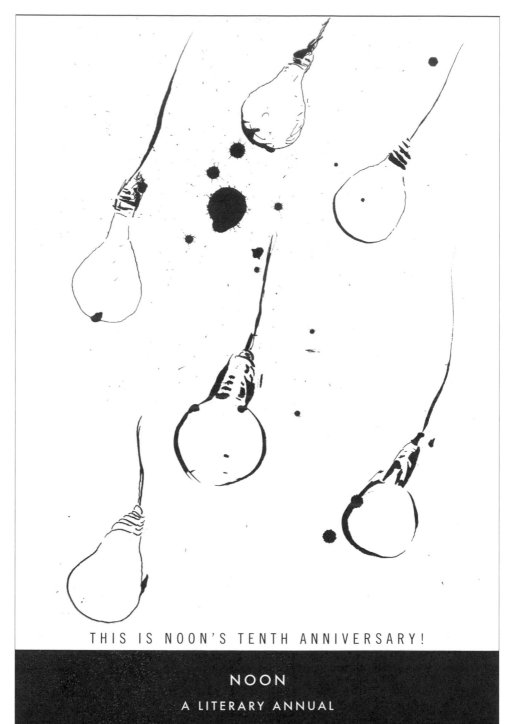

THIS IS NOON'S TENTH ANNIVERSARY!

NOON

A LITERARY ANNUAL

1324 LEXINGTON AVENUE   PMB 298   NEW YORK   NEW YORK   10128

EDITION PRICE $12 DOMESTIC $17 FOREIGN

The editors would like to congratulate the following
Open City *contributors for their recent honors:*

Best American Essays 2008
"Where God Is Glad" by Joe Wenderoth (from *Open City* #23)

Honorable mention: "Satyr Song" by Stanley Moss
(from *Open City* #24)

Best Nonrequired Reading 2008
"The Elegant Rube" by Malerie Willens (from *Open City* #24)

Best Creative Nonfiction 2008
"My First Fairy Tale" by Vijay Seshadri (from *Open City* #23)

The Utne Reader "Gleanings" section, (great writing from the alternative press)
"The Boil" by John O'Connor (from Open City #25)

2008 Whitney Biennial
Matthew Brannon
Roe Ethridge
Ellen Harvey
Karen Kilimnick
Mungo Thomson

2008 Guggenheim Fellow
Sam Lipsyte

2008 Academy of Arts & Letters Award in Literature
Will Eno
Fanny Howe

2008 Academy of Arts & Letters
Harold D. Vursell Memorial Award
Maxine Swann

LINCOLN PLAZA CINEMAS

Six Screens

63RD STREET & BROADWAY
OPPOSITE LINCOLN CENTER
212-757-2280

NICK STONE DESIGN

www.nickstonedesign.com
stone@nickstonedesign.com
tel: 212.995.1863

OPEN

"The Crazy Person" by Mary Gaitskill, "La Vie en Rose" by Hubert Selby Jr., "Cathedral Parkway" by Vince Passaro. Art by Jeff Koons and Devon Dikeou. Cover by Ken Schles, whose *Invisible City* sells for thousands on Ebay. Stan Friedman's poems about baldness and astronomy, Robert Polito on Lester Bangs, Jon Tower's real life letters to astronauts. (Vastly underpriced at $400. Only two copies left.)

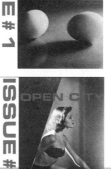

A first glimpse of Martha McPhee; a late burst from Terry Southern. Jaime Manrique's "Twilight at the Equator." Art by Paul Ramirez-Jonas, Kate Milford, Richard Serra. Kip Kotzen's "Skate Dogs," Richard Foreman's "Poetry City" with playful illustrations by Daniel Pinchbeck, David Shields' "Sports" and his own brutal youth. (Ken Schles found the negative of our cover girl on Thirteenth Street and Avenue B. We're still looking for the girl. $25)

Irvine Welsh's "Eurotrash" (his American debut), Richard Yates (from his last, unfinished novel), Patrick McCabe (years before *The Butcher Boy*). Art by Francesca Woodman (with an essay by Betsy Berne), Jacqueline Humphries, Allen Ginsberg, Alix Lambert. A short shot of Lipsyte—"Shed"—not available anywhere else. Plus Alfred Chester's letters to Paul Bowles. Chip Kidd riffs on the Fab Four. (Very few copies left! $25)

Stories by the always cheerful Cyril Connolly ("Happy Deathbeds"), Thomas McGuane, Jim Thompson, Samantha Gillison, Michael Brownstein, and Emily Carter, whose "Glory Goes and Gets Some" was reprinted in *Best American Short Stories.* Art by Julianne Swartz and Peter Nadin. Poems by David Berman and Nick Tosches. Plus Denis Johnson in Somalia. (A monster issue, sales undercut by slightly rash choice of cover art by editors. Get it while you can! $15)

Change or Die
Stories by David Foster Wallace, Siobhan Reagan, Irvine Welsh. Jerome Badanes' brilliant novella, "Change or Die" (film rights still available). Poems by David Berman and Vito Acconci. Plus Helen Thorpe on the murder of Ireland's most famous female journalist, and Delmore Schwartz on T. S. Eliot's squint. (Still sold-out! Wait for e-books to catch on or band together and demand a reprint.)

CITY back issues

Make an investment in your future…
In today's volatile marketplace
you could do worse.

The Only Woman He's Ever Left
Stories by James Purdy, Jocko Weyland, Strawberry Saroyan. Michael Cunningham's "The Slap of Love." Poems by Rick Moody, Deborah Garrison, Monica Lewinsky, Charlie Smith. Art by Matthew Ritchie, Ellen Harvey, Cindy Stefans. Rem Koolhaas project. With a beautiful cover by Adam Fuss. (Only $10 for this blockbuster.)

ISSUE #6

The Rubbed Away Girl
Stories by Mary Gaitskill, Bliss Broyard, and Sam Lipsyte. Art by Jimmy Raskin, Laura Larson, and Jeff Burton. Poems by David Berman, Elizabeth Macklin, Stephen Malkmus, and Will Oldham. (We found some copies in the back of the closet so were able to lower the price! $25 (it *was* $50))

ISSUE #7

Beautiful to Strangers
Stories by Caitlin O'Connor Creevy, Joyce Johnson, and Amine Wefali, back when her byline was Zaitzeff (now the name of her organic sandwich store at Nassau & John Streets—go there for lunch!). Poems by Harvey Shapiro, Jeffrey Skinner, and Daniil Kharms. Art by David Robbins, Liam Gillick, and Elliott Puckette. Piotr Uklanski's cover is a panoramic view of Queens, shot from the top of the World Trade Center in 1998. ($10)

ISSUE #8

Bewitched
Stories by Jonathan Ames, Said Shirazi, and Sam Lipsyte. Essays by Geoff Dyer and Alexander Chancellor, who hates rabbit. Poems by Chan Marshall, Lucy Anderson, and Edvard Munch on intimate and sensitive subjects. Art by Karen Kilimnick, Giuseppe Penone, Mark Leckey, Maurizio Cattelan, and M.I.M.E. (Our bestselling issue. ($10))

ISSUE #9

Editors' Issue
Previously demure editors publish themselves. Enormous changes at the last minute. Stories by Robert Bingham, Thomas Beller, Daniel Pinchbeck, Joanna Yas, Adrian Dannatt, Kip Kotzen, Geoffrey O' Brien, Lee Smith, Amanda Gersh, and Jocko Weyland. Poems by Tony Torn. Art by Nick Stone, Meghan Gerety, and Alix Lambert. (Years later, Ken Schles's cover photo appears on a Richard Price novel.) ($10)

ISSUE #10

OPEN

CITY

Please send a check or
money order payable to:

Open City, Inc.
270 Lafayette Street, Suite 1412
New York, NY 10012

For credit-card orders, see www.opencity.org.

I wait, I wait.
A brilliant outtake from Robert Bingham's *Lightning on the Sun*. Ryan Kenealy on the girl who ran off with the circus; Nick Tosches on Proust. Art by Allen Ruppersberg, David Bunn, Nina Katchadourian, Matthew Higgs, and Matthew Brannon. Stories by Evan Harris, Lewis Robinson, Michael Sledge, and Bruce Jay Friedman. Rick Rofihe feels Marlene. Poetry by Dana Goodyear, Nathaniel Bellows, and Kevin Young. ($10)

They're at it again.
Lara Vapnyar's "There Are Jews in My House," Chuck Kinder on Dagmar. Special poetry section guest edited by Honor Moore, including C. K. Williams, Victoria Redel, Eamon Grennan, and Carolyn Forché. Art by Stu Mead, Christoph Heemann, Jason Fox, Herzog film star Bruno S., and Sophie Toulouse, whose "Sexy Clowns" project has become a "character note for [our] intentions" (says the *Literary Magazine Review*). See what all the fuss is about. ($10)

I Want to Be Your Shoebox
Susan Chamandy on Hannibal's elephants and hockey, Mike Newirth's noirish "Semiprecious." Rachel Blake's "Elephants" (an unintentional elephant theme emerges). Poetry by Catherine Dowman and Rodney Jack. Art by Viggo Mortensen, Alix Lambert, Marcellus Hall, Mark Solotroff, and Alaskan Pipeline polar bear cover by Jason Middlebrook (we're still trying to figure out what the bear had for lunch). ($10)

Post Hoc Ergo Propter Hoc
Stories by Jason Brown, Bryan Charles, Amber Dermont, Luis Jaramillo, Dawn Raffel, Bryan Charles, Nina Shope, and Alicia Erian. Robert Olen Butler's severed heads. Poetry by Jim Harrison, Sarah Gorham, Trevor Dannatt, Matthew Rohrer & Joshua Beckman, and Harvey Shapiro. Art by Bill Adams, Juliana Ellman, Sally Ross, and George Rush. Eerie, illustrated children's story by Rick Rofihe and Thomas Roberston. Saucy cover by Wayne Gonzales. ($10)

Homecoming
"The Egg Man" a novella by Scott Smith, author of *A Simple Plan* (screenplay and book); Ryan Kenealy does God's math; an unpublished essay by Paul Bowles. Stories by Rachel Sherman, Sam Shaw, and Maxine Swann. Art by Shelter Serra and William McCurtin (of *Story of My Scab* and *Elk* fame). Poems by Anthony Roberts, Honor Moore, and David Lehman. ($10)

OPEN CITY

back issues

Ballast
Matthew Zapruder's "The Pajamaist," David Nutt's "Melancholera," fiction by Rachel Sherman, a Nick Tosches poem, Phillip Lopate's "Tea at the Plaza," David A. Fitschen on life on tour as a roadie. Poetry by Matt Miller and Alex Phillips. Art by Molly Smith, Robert Selwyn, Miranda Lichtenstein, Lorenzo Petrantoni, Billy Malone, and M Blash. ($10)

Fiction/Nonfiction
A special double-sided issue featuring fiction by Sam Lipsyte, Jerry Stahl, Herbert Gold, Leni Zumas, Matthew Kirby, Jonathan Baumbach, Ann Hillesland, Manuel Gonzales, and Leland Pitts-Gonzales. Nonfiction by Priscilla Becker, Vestal McIntyre, Eric Pape, Jocko Weyland, and Vince Passaro. ($10)

Prose by Poets
Prose and poetry by Anne Sexton, Nick Flynn, Jim Harrison, Wayne Koestenbaum, Joe Wenderoth, Glyn Maxwell, Rebecca Wolff, Vijay Seshadri, Jerome Badanes, Deborah Garrison, Jill Bialosky, Cynthia Kraman, Max Blagg, Thorpe Moeckel, Greg Purcell, Rodney Jack, Hadara Bar-Nadav, and Nancy Willard. ($10)

Secret Engines
Three debuts: Malerie Willens, Gerard Coletta, and Ian Martin. Stanley Moss as a bronze satyr; heavy breathing with Jeff Johnson. Stories by Jonathan Baumbach, Erin Brown, Wayne Conti, James Hannaham, and Claire Keegan. Poetry by Mark Hartenbach, Alex Lemon, and Baron Wormser. Art by Amy Bird, Jay Batlle, Noelle Tan, and Doug Shaeffer. ($10)

High Wire
Robert Stone's epic novella (set midway between the reigns of Elvis Presley and Bill Clinton); stories by Jonathan Ames, Charles Bukowski, Rivka Galchen, Jon Groebner, Said Shirazi, Giuseppe O. Longo, and Sarah Gardner Borden. Poetry by Howard Altmann, Jennifer Richter, and Ben Carlton Turner. Art by Ellen Harvey, Michael Scoggins, Mark C, and Duncan Hannah. ($10)

In memoriam

RODNEY JACK

1964–2008

In memoriam

DAVID FOSTER WALLACE

1962–2008

The Long Ride Back Home

Mohammed Naseehu Ali

BEFORE THEIR DEPARTURE FROM BOLGATANGA'S LORRY STATION
Abure had told his son, Sando, that they would be on the road for
only two days. But the journey was now in its third day, and from
hushed conversations Sando overheard between the driver's mate
and other disgruntled passengers, they still had at least another day
of travel before they reached Kumasi, the big city down south.

The M.A.N. Diesel-headed lorry was packed with sheep, yams,
goats, guinea fowl, cows, bags of millet, bales of hand-woven *fugu*
fabric, and about two dozen humans. The lorry's long rectangular
hull, divided in two sections contained the beasts in one, while the
food, human, and merchandize cargos were held in the other. With
little room below, about half of the passengers had to perch on the
food cargo—their heads extending beyond the lorry's wooden frame,
in danger of being tossed to the ground any time the driver dodged a
pot hole.

The lorry traveled at donkey-trot pace. To make matters worse,
the driver stopped at every village along the Bolgatanga-Kumasi
highway, to either off-load or replenish his human and animal cargos. Sometimes the driver would disappear for hours, visiting a relative or a mistress, as some of the passengers insinuated. Some of the
passengers would roam about the town or village to buy food. Others

would bring down their animals, so they could graze in roadside bushes and to also defecate before they loaded them back onto the vehicle. There were three other boys and a girl in the lorry who were about Sando's age, and Sando had hoped he and they would perhaps form a friendship and play together; but all the kids acted as if they had sworn a vow of silence.

Between his chest and his raised knee Sando clutched a rubber bag that contained his only possessions: two worn out *obroniwawu* T-shirts, a sleep cloth, a pair of hole-in-the-knee khaki trousers, a straw hat, and a cache of creative, handmade playthings that included his favorite and most valuable belonging—the catapult he used for hunting small rodents and birds. The catapult, a gift from his maternal grandfather when Sando turned nine, was a testament of the old man's confidence in Sando's hunting ability. Sando's marksmanship, the accuracy with which he nailed grass cutters was so superb the grandfather nicknamed Sando "the shooting wonder of the savannah." Many times during the trip, Sando fingered the contents one by one, to make sure the catapult was exactly where he had put it when he had packed up the bag.

The air in the lorry was laden with the putrid smell of cow dung, the incessant high-pitched quack of guinea fowl, the odor of unwashed human bodies, the acrid, sustained stench of oozes from open, untreated cutlass wounds the passengers had suffered back on their village farms, and finally, the odious and murderous reek of hunger. Shortly after the lorry had left the station, a bitter, sour, and nauseating taste rose from the linings of Sando's colicky intestines. It made its way up his throat and then to his tongue, where it lodged throughout the journey.

Barely two years before this, Abure had taken Alaraba, Sando's older sister by three years, to Kumasi, where she worked in the household of one of the city's richest men. At least that was Abure's claim. Abure had also told Sando and his mother that the rich man Alaraba worked for had been so impressed by her diligence that he had enrolled her in a night school, to learn how to read and write.

Whether this was true or not, Sando had no means of knowing, as both he and his mother had not heard from Alaraba herself since she was taken away.

Sando was one of thirteen children Abure had sired among five women. Like his father, Sando was short and wiry, though where the boy was as perky and nimble as a gazelle, the father was as slow as a tortoise, and when in conversation blinked slowly, like one who had seen a witch in broad daylight. Sando, as if to make up for not inheriting his father's blinking-eye syndrome, stammered when he spoke.

Sando's father had never married any of his children's mothers. The tradition of his Frafra people, a largely animist population with few Christians and Muslims among them, demanded from a potential suitor a dowry of four hefty cows and a lump sum of money before one was given a wife. A perpetual lazy bone to begin with, Abure certainly didn't have the means to afford even a cow's leg, let alone four bulls. He, like many men in the Frafra north, relied on the alternative, concubine arrangement, which conveniently suited Abure's amorphous lifestyle. He came to the women, impregnated them, and left. But as soon as the children reached the ages of ten or eleven, Abure returned and snatched them from their mothers. He took them down south, to work as house servants. With the monthly wages Abure collected for the children's labor, he purchased mosquito coils and bicycle spare parts, which he sold up north for much bigger profits. With such neat arrangement Abure couldn't have asked for more from the god of his ancestors, to whom he now and then offered libations for lifting him out of the perpetual destitution in the north.

Five days after Sando and his father had set off from Bolgatanga, the lorry crawled into a parking slot at the infamous Kumasi Kejetia Lorry Park. As Sando and his father meandered their way through the city's humongous central market—where they delivered Abure's guinea fowls to his customers—the young boy fantasized living in one of the multistory buildings he had seen from the lorry's top when they drove into the city. *A real concrete and block house with real aluminum roofing sheets and glass windows and real doors and a mattress for me to sleep on.*

Sando imagined his first three days in this sequence: Day One—take a bath, eat and sleep; Day Two—visit his sister; Day Three—go with his father to find a placement for him at the local elementary school, a promise Abure had made to the boy and his mother. What both mother and son didn't know was that Abure had months ago made a promise to a Kumasi Muslim man named Abdul, that he would get him a good workerboy next time he traveled up north. "Babu Shakka," Abure had sworn. "In Allah's name, I will bring you a veryvery obedient and hard-working boy. And this one is my very own son."

Like most men on Zongo Street, Abdul had multiple wives. Though Islamic shari-ah allowed Muslim men to take up to four wives, Abdul, cognizant of his limited means, had married just three. With as many as a dozen and a half children from his three wives and with no real vocation—other than being a *dillali* for pawned goods transactions on the street—Abdul himself was desperate for a househelp that could serve the dual purpose of servant and income-generator in one. Moreover, Abdul's second wife, Asanata, had been nagging him for a servant, to help with the family's increasing chores.

"Thank you, thank you, thank you!" Abdul beamed when Abure appeared at his door mouth with Sando. "This must be the son you promised me, ko?"

"*Babu shakka,*" answered Abure in the affirmative. He inhaled his perpetual smoke pipe as deeply as if his very life depended on it.

"He looks like you, ko?" said Abdul.

"*Babu Shakka.* And I promise you he will work wellwell for you and your wife and your family."

After a period of sustained bargaining for Sando's services, the two men agreed on seventy cedis per month, and Abure demanded that Abdul paid the first three months upfront. The haggling was carried out in Hausa, a tongue in which the father spoke only in adulterated pidgin, and of which Sando understood just a handful. Abure looked at his son and grinned, exposing his tobacco-stained teeth. Though confused, Sando bowed his head, unwittingly acquiescing to the deal between the men. In less than five hours of Sando's arrival in Kumasi, the transaction of leasing him into bondage had concluded. Sando was further confused, saddened even; the whole transaction reminded him of another that had transpired just an hour ago in the market, in which his father and his customers had haggled for the price of his guinea fowl.

Perhaps Abure had sensed that Sando was no fool after all, and that the son may have understood what was unraveling. He drew Sando aside and whispered to him: "You will start school in a few months, boy, when school reopens. But first you have to work to raise the money for the fees, you hear me so?" Sando did what was expected of an obedient son and nodded, though by now he had began to develop a deep mistrust of his father. Abure left a few minutes later, promising he would take Sando to see his sister "when I return in two months time."

Barely seconds after Abure had left the vizier's house, Asanata, Abdul's second wife, handed Sando a sleeping mat, and guided him to one of the two rooms in the *zaure*—a long and narrow passageway that led to the house's open courtyard. Aside from being used for storage, the zaure room assigned to Sando also served as the mess hall for boys in the compound. It was there they took naps in the afternoon, played games, and took refuge at night when they ran afoul of their parents.

Sando looked around the darkly lit room in apprehensive fear. He untied the rubber bag and pulled out his catapult. He did a thorough inspection of the contraption, then slid it in the front pocket of his khaki trousers. He tied the bag, which later became his pillow, and placed it next to the mat. As Sando sat still on the floor, he heard Asanata screaming, "Sando! Hey, Sando! Saaandooo!" Sando answered, "A, A, Anti," and dashed out of the room into the court-yard, responding to the call for what was the first of a million errands he would run for the Abduls and other families in the compound.

The vizier's house was a rectangular behemoth with more than thirty rooms, three open kitchens, and half a dozen chicken coops. Not counting the Abduls, the house contained eleven other nuclear families, and a total of eighty-three inhabitants. And very soon after Sando's arrival, his name was on everybody's lips. "Go buy me this, Sando." "Sando, go and wash my clothes." "Here, Sando, take these shoes and polish them." "Sando go climb the tree and fetch us some mangoes." He was ordered left and right by the old and the young alike. "Sando, you bastard, didn't you hear me call you?" the rascals would bark. Poor Sando would dash toward his commander with a "Sosososorry, Papa" or "Sosososorry, Anti." As his father had instruct-ed, Sando called every female "Anti" and every male "Papa", no mat-ter their age.

Sando's day started as early as the first cock crow. His immediate set of tasks included sweeping Asanata's verandah, filling up the hun-dred-gallon drum in front of her quarters with water he fetched from the public tap outside the house, washing and sanitizing the sheep's pen, and finally feeding the animals their breakfast of salted plantain peel and water. Then it was time for Sando to start a charcoal fire, boil bath water for Asanata and her three children, before he set off to buy *koko da kose* for the family's breakfast. No porridge and beancake for Sando; he was given the surplus, hardened tuo from the previous night. And on the many occasions that Asanata didn't have any sup-pie for him, she would casually say, "There is no food for you this morning." To this, Sando would nod and bow his head.

At mid-morning Sando washed the family's dirty linens, polished their dusty shoes, and ironed their wrinkled garments. By the time he was done with these chores, around one o'clock, Asanata had already bottled her *biyan-tankwa* for Sando to take to the market square, where he hawked the ginger brew until sundown. This business brought in a decent income to Asanata—enough to buy food ingredients for the family's supper and to pay for Sando's monthly wage.

Sando's only free time came after *lissha*, when the families had completed the final obligatory Muslim worship, and had gathered in little clusters in front of their verandahs to eat supper. Sando and the other worker boys and worker girls in the compound ate only after their masters and mistresses had finished eating. Sando accepted whatever portion was given to him with gratitude and retreated to the zaure, where he ate in silence. The food was never enough for him, so he topped it with lots of water, and also with the crumbs he sometimes got from other families—their way of compensation for the many errands Sando ran for them.

Sando worked all day and every day, and was unofficially allowed only two free days in a year: the day of the Feast of Ramadan and the day of the Feast of Sacrifice, the two major Muslim holidays. And only on those days was Sando left in relative peace. He would sit in the zaure room as the streetfolks began the festival of eating, dancing, and gift-giving that marked the end of the monthlong Ramadan fasting, and would also do the same during the Feast of Sacrifice, when the city's Muslim residents slaughtered thousands of cattle, sheep, and goats, to mark the end of the pilgrimage to Mecca. When would his own eternal fast and sacrifice end? Sando wondered during those festive days, as music and laughter poured in through the window.

Sando was lying in the zaure room on the day of his third Feast of Sacrifice at the vizier's house when three boys barged in and quickly locked the door behind them.

"Bend down," said Asim, the oldest of the gang.

"Whawhawha . . . what now?" asked Sando. He was accustomed to all sorts of pranks and bullying from the compound boys, especially when he returned late from their errands. But Sando didn't remember running afoul of any of the boys lately. He asked again, "Whawhawha, what have I done, now?"

"I say bend down," came Asim's menacing response, followed by a knuckle to Sando's head.

Confused, Sando laughed, but still refused to do Asim's bidding.

"Habahaba . . . haba, whawhawhat . . . what have I done thithithi . . . this time, hah, hah?" asked Sando, who tried to laugh his way out of his predicament.

"I say bend down!" Asim said, and slapped Sando on the head again. He instructed the other boys to hold Sando's arms, and before the poor worker boy knew what was happening, the boys had pulled his half-torn knickers down to his knees. Sando put up a struggle and managed to free himself from their grip.

"Whawhawha . . . what is allall, all this now? I don't like this o!" sputtered Sando. The boys suddenly burst into laughter. But it took Sando a few seconds to realize that they were mocking his *koteboto*, which was an object of derision and even contempt on Zongo Street. "He is koteboto, he is koteboto," they hissed and giggled. Sando quickly covered his nakedness with his open palms.

"Now turn," Asim said angrily, as if the discovery of Sando's uncircumcised penis had further incensed his ire. He grabbed Sando's arm, then twisted it violently. Sando succumbed and lay on his belly. With his nose touching the floor, Sando blew dust into the air, only for him to inhale it again.

Asim quickly climbed on top of the servant boy, his erection blindly seeking the mouth of Sando's anus. Sando tried to move his body sideways, to thwart Asim's efforts, but he was overwhelmed by the other boys' grip on his arms and legs. Powerless, Sando gave up and could only imagine himself a lamb being sacrificed to Allah. A violent pain shot through Sando's body as Asim forced his way through. Sando screamed wildly, but nobody outside heard his cry. A commotion much more important to the compound of the vizier's house was taking place then: a cow being led to the slaughter pit had somehow managed to set itself free. The beast ran amok, knocking down everything and everyone in its path, while the hysterical housefolks ran helter skelter for their lives. The compound was filled with the moos and bleating of the other soon-to-be-sacrificed animals who—in their exclamations—appeared to encourage the aberrant cow to elude its pursuers.

Though Asim and his cohorts were oblivious to what was exactly taking place outside, the loud noises certainly encouraged them to carry on.

"Haba, haba, please. Whawha, what have I done? I bebe, beg you, now," Sando pleaded, as the pain exploded. Asim continued, gasping with each stroke, while the two boys—amid suppressed laughter—hissed, "*I-mishi! I-mishi!*", urging him to give Sando some more.

Who Sando had been before this encounter was now light years in the past. Personally, Sando had hardly thought about sex. He would sit and listen quietly whenever the boys in the compound chatted about their adolescent fantasies and boasted the number of girls they had bedded. In his present agony he wondered if women, when penetrated by men, suffered the same pain he was experiencing. Sando had heard that Kokobiro, the transvestite chop bar owner on Yalwa Street, slept with men at night, and Sando had often wondered how a man could sleep with a fellow man. *How could anybody enjoy this ordeal? Why are they doing this to me?* Though Sando's body convulsed in shock, he feared he might put himself in even worse trouble if he shouted for help. Master would likely take the boys' words over mine, he thought. And, besides, wasn't a servant to obey? Always. He thought of his father's whip and of the distant possibility of school.

After a couple of minutes or so, Asim pulled away from Sando's rear. He was all sweaty and gasping for breath. Calm had also been restored to the vizier's house's compound. The defiant cow had been apprehended, but not until it had dragged its chasers all the way to Zerikyi Road and had triumphantly knocked over the tables and food trays of many vendors and hawkers along its way. The captors flogged the crazy cow as they dragged it back to the house, in blind retaliation of the pain it had put them through. Also, the two dozen or so cattle, goats, and sheep slated for sacrifice had all been silenced by the fawa's blade. The zaure and the large porch outside were smeared with blood as young adults carried the animals into the courtyard, where they were skinned and hanged out to dry in the sun.

With little noise coming from outside, the boys thought it wise to leave, lest they be caught if Sando screamed again. They snuck out of the room, and left Sando curled up on the dusty straw mat. Sweat poured from every pore. His breathing, short and irregular, prevented him from crying. He made an attempt to get up, but his backside hurt so badly he slumped back onto the floor. The sharp, burning sensation around his anus was followed by an oozing down his thighs. He rubbed his fingers on his skin and lifted his hands to the light. What Sando saw was a mixture of blood and a watery, milky fluid, which dripped from him the way water escapes a faulty tap. With a rag he found on the floor, Sando wiped off the mess, and with his backside still on the floor, he slowly managed to put on his knickers.

The following day was the festival's "meat distributing day," when the dried meat of the sacrificed animals was shared among family members and friends and poor folks in the community. Sando was given a few pieces of beef and the innards of a goat, which he spent hours cleaning, to get rid of the feces hidden in the animal's intestines. Later that day, as Sando joyfully made himself a pot of stew with his share, Asim and the two boys approached him. "Let me tell you," said Asim. "If you dare open your mouth about what we did, the whole street would know about your koteboto." Sando swore he would not say a word to anybody. But the boys, assured that Sando would keep his word, raped him several times more, taking turns with each encounter. They stopped only when Asim, who was sixteen, got his first girlfriend. At one point, Sando considered waylaying his assailants near the football park and attacking them with his catapult. But he backed out in the end, afraid that his most-prized possession may be confiscated if he used it in that manner.

Then in the eighth year of Sando's arrival in Kumasi, a group of military officers toppled the country's government. The revolt that ensued after the coup d'état was very popular among the nation's poor masses, who chanted: LET THE BLOOD FLOW! The blood of the small elite class that had oppressed, and made destitute of, the nation's majority. Sando, nineteen at the time, took advantage of the four-month-long chaotic and "freedom for the masses" euphoria that swept the nation. He fled the vizier's house.

Sando relocated to the Asawasi market, to the east of the city. There he found work as *kayaye* and also as errand boy for the rich cola-nut merchants. Very soon Sando was making four times more than his father had made on his behalf. But freedom, as they say, has its perils. Before long, Sando fell into bad company at the market, where he slept in big storage rooms with other migrant workers, in whose midst existed many miscreants. He took to drinking pito, a favorite among his fellow northerners. This locally produced brandy heralded an ecstatic, if delusional, period for "the worker boy from the vizier's house," as he was sometimes called. Sando truly felt that the revolution that followed the coup d'état, for better or for worse, and for all the killings and public floggings of citizens, was waged to free people like him, to give them back their lives—to restore their collective dignity.

Yet, for all of Sando's newly acquired autonomy, sex eluded him to his grave. Apart from what happened at the vizier's house, Sando never had any real sexual encounter—not even the prostitutes on whom he wasted some of his hard earned income. He came very close to fulfilling this desire, once, when Suraju—Zongo Street's notorious swindler and *drinkard*, connected him with a woman at Efie Nkwanta, the old whorehouse on Bompata Road. But, the girl fled the room naked on seeing Sando's koteboto, considered ill omen by the city's prostitutes.

When Sando turned twenty-one, he developed a peculiar, if mysterious disease. It started with a few boils on his left thigh, but within ten days of the appearance of the first boil, Sando looked like a giant boil himself; the affliction now covered his buttocks, legs, and upper body. His face, body, and legs swelled as if he was being pumped daily with a toxic liquid. The boils would break open, releasing a mire that attracted flies to his body. Tormented by this unknown malady, and with no place in the city to call home, Sando headed for the only refuge he knew—the vizier's house. After their initial anger and the curses shot at him for running away from them, Abdul and Assanata, fearful of the karmaic implications of turning away a human in dire need of help, had a change of heart. They pleaded with other folks in the compound to allow Sando the usage of the zaure room. The housefolks agreed, and emptied the room of the bags of maize and konkonti they had in storage. Soon afterward they and their children avoided the room altogether.

A decade after his arrival in Kumasi, Sando had yet to set eyes on his sister. And as for Abure, the last time Sando saw him was when the father trekked to the Asawasi market not long after Sando's escape from the vizier's house. The father tried then to convince Sando to come with him back to Zuarungu, promising to make him partner in a farm he had started. Sando had flatly refused the offer, and had boldly reminded his father of his many deceptions. Powerless against a now grown Sando, Abure had departed in shame. Sando drank himself to stupor that night, a celebration of the fact that for the first time in his life he had mustered enough strength and courage to say "No."

A decade after his arrival in Kumasi, Sando had lost all but only one of the original possessions contained in the little rubber bag he had carried into the city. The catapult. It remained the only surviving link between Sando and his mother and his two sisters and his grandfather and his village. Though Sando never used the catapult in Kumasi, it always imbued him with the hope that he would one day return home to Zuarungu—to the Savannah and its exotic birds; to the lizards he and his childhood friends chased and shot with their catapults; to the nocturnal calls of the black cricket, who at dusk emerges from its hiding place under the logs and burrows to sing and celebrate its mere survival for yet another night. It was in such dreamlike state that Sando's hopes dissipated into the reality of his death as he slept one night in the zaure room. In his final seconds, Sando believed he was embarking on a journey, a rather long one, back to Zuarungu. And unlike the rickety, smelly lorry that had a decade earlier brought him to the city, *he*, this time, traveled in luxury, held aloft by white-feathered angels, who sang the songs of his childhood as they accompanied him, *the shooting wonder of the Savannah*, on his long ride back home.

I squeezed past her for the door,

remembering what Errol Flynn said:

the woman always chooses,

it just looks the other way.

(Alcalay, page 81)

Math Poem

Priscilla Becker

Because it will not snow
we calculate In inches
our quietism.

The whiteness of our eyes diminishes
as from the year's prophetic
poison, our long drag finishes.

I found it democratic
leaving sloughings of ourselves
in every coffee shop, pseudo-

scientific. The tally under-
whelms. But still I collect
specimen, I line the shelves.

The virtual calendar subtracts.
Examining my maps: no sex
till Nova Scotia I predict.

Each year about this time I resurrect
my vows to vultures, cults,
the obliterative X.

Midwestern

After what was likely half
my life I began to understand
what was required:

abstinence from mood, refusal
of the bundled nerves.

Therefore when all the clichés
gather in the bars at noon
you find yourself a professional
distance away

And is that why machine age
artifacts spread like wildfires
in the west—the sound

of hammering, metals
pressed flat

On almost every corner
there's a version of the song
—sour twang,
reworked words

Therefore you find yourself
in lessened light, walking off
the afternoon.

Priscilla Becker

afters

at long last the feeling
like a night with some
stars, a day with the keys
home left home
as though you'd been
    a mime

you don't recognize
everything clean
but the part of you that builds
and accumulates has been
erased and you can start
over, not over but
before, not before but
with ugly knowing

you've moved across
the red grey landscape
and you can act now
partly innocent of yourself

Desert

When we were a babe
full of empty roads,
hanging precipice,
a babe of particular
innocence—
for it is not as if
we did not know

When we were small
with the small fear growing,
we looked into the knees of it
and shook with cactus
knowledge—

Older
and more solid
than our years. Each day
fools us with its newness,
we make promises,
the needles point
to the stone monument.

Priscilla Becker

Hatred of Men with Blond Eyebrows

It was not without omen—
the owl at the back
of the lecture hall, the dream
of old men in white bathing caps.

    But I was arrogant
    about that.

The doorway seemed a momentary
place, but soon I made a nest—
pink styrofoam, calipers, rubber bands,
sciroccos of fur

I think I'd be judged if I left.
But there's a deception I know:
the body can move on its own.

Down in Tarzana, the last Orange Julius in southern California finally shuts its doors. (Specktor, page 59)

Dick

Kirsty Gunn

I WAS STILL FRESH FROM MY PARENTS' DIVORCE WHEN MY FATHER
gave me a car and taught me to drive. It was just before school broke
up for the summer and getting hot, and I was too young to be out on
the road on my own but my father knew all kinds of people in our
small town and he had, as he put it, "conversations." Like he had them
with his ladies and his friends, certain conversations about money
deals and business debts, so my father could get what he wanted in
his life, so he could get his way.

Until that time of the car, though, these kinds of things hadn't
occurred to me. I was somewhat held back, you might say, was the
reason—made younger than my years by my father and the way he
carried on. That's what my brother Michael said. We were both kind
of wrecked, him and I, by our old dad and our mother leaving home
and moving abroad and it turned out we wouldn't see her again for
another fifteen years. So I may be living in the world like everyone
else with my own profession and my little tidy flat, but part of me still
is that same girl from back then, learning to use the clutch then go
first gear, second. Slowly driving on my own down the street where
we lived.

There was a boy next door who I used to watch from my bedroom
window and dream that one day he might look up as I came carefully
past him, practicing in that too-fancy brand new convertible of mine.

He had a car of his own, an old lovely car, and would be out in front of his house working on it, an older boy with long blond hair that straggled down his back and the way he stood there in the sun in those beaten up old jeans he wore and T-shirts that hung just anyhow over his body . . . Even now the feelings I have about him mean I could never say his name.

My father didn't know anything about this. I didn't think then he thought of me that way. He just had the driving instructor pick me up after school each day and start the lesson there—as I turned the ignition and put the car in gear. Then we drove back to the house and my father paid him and made me go up and down the streets myself, around the block and over the hill by the shops. Certain times he even came with me, my father, that's how much he wanted me to drive. He'd be sitting right beside me in the tiny seat of the car he'd bought for me as a gift, telling me this way or that, giving instructions on what to do at a set of lights . . . but always looking at his watch, too, and wanting to get back—"to some little chickie he had waiting upstairs" were my brother's words. Or something else he needed to do. Still, those few times with him were times I felt close, when he said "clutch now" or "reverse." And even on the days he didn't come, I thought I could sense his affection in the way he would wave me off goodbye. As if he was pleased to think that soon I'd be in that car forever and I'd be driving away.

So the two weeks passed before school broke up and twice I went out and the boy in the street was waiting, kind of—is how I wanted to believe it was. Hanging around by his car as I drove past him in my own. And twice I saw him look up as I passed, push the yellow hair back clean from his face as I went from second gear into first while time seemed to slow down and then stop, with the blue of that sweet boy's eyes upon me. Thinking, in that moment, how it might be to get someone to love you. To let your mouth go wide open so another person could come in.

But I didn't see the boy in the street again that summer—or if I did, I don't remember. Because something went wrong with the car—

something, my father said, that was to do with the engine and that it would need to go in to the garage straight away. "There are often problems" he said "with these little convertibles. You can get a bit of trouble with the braking, stopping suddenly." I remember exactly how he looked at me then, my old handsome dad. He was on his way, I remember, out the kitchen door. "I'll take it in to the garage today," he said, "and you can pick it up later, after school. Dick's a friend of mine. He does the work himself on all my cars. He'll do it in a day and you can drive it home after on your own."

That was a long time ago, that morning when everything changed for me like it had changed for my brother before me but he never talked about it and now he never left his room, just stayed in there in the dark. A lifetime, you might say, and a day with all of my life locked inside it, a secret I would never tell. Even my mother, when I finally saw her, was not someone I could reveal myself to, to show myself that way. When we met, after all that time of her being gone we were both of us strangers. But I do remember how my mother said "You don't surround yourself with certain kinds of people and not feel the consequences," is what she said. "Except your father, well . . . he just found a way of not letting himself feel the effects of anything he did. Or what those so-called 'friends' of his might do."

She was right, of course. For the last time I drove was that day coming back from Dick's garage, and my father, as long as he lived, never did ask me why. Though he was the one who'd fixed it to turn out for me that way. He'd given me the car after all, when I was too young, arranged that it would need to go in to the garage that day, and that the garage would be empty, with no cars at all, no men, no customers around when I walked in to the empty yard. There was the sign RICHARD CLARKE AND CO. LIMITED over the entrance but only one man there in the dark office waiting. *Dick's a friend of mine.* "And I've been waiting for you," he said.

And so I'm left here with the memory of it, fitting in the pieces, all grown up now and old, and my poor brother still in that place where they keep him like he's a child. And my father long dead and the girlfriends gone and my mother, after she spoke with me that day, never did come back . . . And you try to understand, don't you? They say: write down your stories and you'll come to a kind of learning. Write all the way to the ending. Read the story out loud.

But what I'm left with at the end is no different to what I had when I began: a set of keys, a "conversation." A gift. Some kind of start but really with no words to follow. And so you know why there's something wrong with me by now, why the boy in the road is a dream, why my brother stays inside. Why I don't come up to people, don't get close. Something that comes from that mess all over my clothing that day, of oil and other stuff, from that minute of my father walking toward me in the hall when I got home . . . After all that happened, all that he let happen . . . Calling out to me and smiling . . . with some fresh lovely shirt on, and he says "Hi honey, everything gone okay?"

That comes from knowing then what he knew, that he'd given me too, I was one of his "gifts." My old powerful handsome dad. But was never, ever going to say. What had happened. What debt I'd paid. What Dick had done.

Crossing Chilmark Pond

Elizabeth Schmidt

That August morning they woke in the dark.
A girl looked through the night for her mother,
who rowed her and her brother in a gray-blue boat
across a weedy pond to a bar of sand
that stretched, like a great curved hand, holding sky
above churning pond and endless ocean.

She could see how the world came from the ocean
and yet still felt the pull of the dark
water shifting under the light-streaked sky.
The outline of her rocking mother
whispered of what they'd see from the sand
after they all helped unload the boat.

They packed so much into that old rowboat,
things they never brought to the ocean;
a rocker, a torn net, their dog whose coat collected sand,
props for the photo shoot they planned in the dark.
The even, dripping strokes of her mother
made a path under the milky sky,

as the stars slipped back into the sky,
and when they landed, the scrape of the boat
startled her sleeping brother. Their mother
rubbed his head and studied the ocean
through her lens: now greens swirled with the dark,
and water leaped, slapped at the sand

while all around them light danced—sand
shimmered, sparked under the blushing sky
as it rose from the ocean's weakened dark.
The girl helped lift the rocker from the boat,
saw its motion, known for twelve years, in the ocean,
and wearing a powder-blue nightgown (her mother's)

she felt small, felt like and unlike her mother,
as its lace neck sagged and she tripped in the sand
on its trailing hem. Their dog sniffed the ocean.
Her brother lifted the net to the nectarine sky,
and their mother photographed the empty boat:
lit from behind, it was flat and dark,

and set like a cup between ocean and sky.
The girl watched her mother from the chair in the sand
and listened to the once-dark pond lap at their boat.

Elizabeth Schmidt

Quiet Comfort

I.

Noise into sound
yields quiet.

That was the gist
of the business plan.

Start with a noise you can't stand
then fabricate a sound of opposite polarity—

finely attuned
and perfectly counter.

Imagine half a tremulous
Venn diagram

conjured up to cancel out
the original offending noise.

That jackhammer outside your window?
Turn the dial on your machine,

it vibrates with equal hostility,
emitting harsh

OPEN CITY

percussive sounds—
hmm, no, that's no good,

let's make the countersound
slow and harp-like, absorptive . . .

At any rate, overhead,
sound meets noise,

leaving nothing
in the ear's calm canals

where the bird bones settle
in return to thought.

Someone I know
lost a fortune in this.

Noise Cancellation
stalled in development.

He was ruined.
I never got why,

couldn't ask,
was left to figure—

at the occasional party,
we spoke too eagerly of our kids.

II.

"Hearing less lets you hear more . . ."
That got my attention on the radio,

while driving out of the city yesterday.
The river winked as it flowed past,

the sun peeked over
glassy high-rise land

named in twenty-foot brass caps
for the world's loudest billionaire.

Voiceover guy beckoned,
noise reduction, it can be yours,

you can, you should,
if you travel, you must

get these noise-canceling headphones.
You'll hear pure music for the first time.

I was off—head framed
by pillowy transport shells

designed to keep
disturbance at bay

with their own
customized disturbance,

whorled white noise
all cupped up, so

fluttering catalogs,
chimes and coughs and howling kids

even the engine screaming,
we are taking off!

—everything, gets whisked
away by QuietComfort®

leaving ample
nutshell space

for your private sound track,
for your listening pleasure,

ringing unperturbed
and fathomless.

III.

Two horses pulling the same driver
long to move in opposite ways:

the heavy bay paws earth,
splits rocks with his wild hooves

the other with lambent mane, wants air—
to her ground is just for taking off.

The driver reins in both,
keeps them running, side by side,

they feel the bit
yet still believe,

we could run free—
grace as restrained potency.

Elizabeth Schmidt

Take that roadside maple
I almost missed at noon today:

the wind was the driver,
turning each winedark leaf

two sides, contrasting,
flashing, wave after wave

in silent fire/dusk,
dusk/fire symphony—

if the sides were the same,
the wind couldn't work,

and I'd have missed
that tree, which,

among other things,
brings to mind

the Southern Man's song
about the Cadillac,

a wheel in a ditch
and a wheel on the track,

and this, in turn,
enlivens the scenic overlooks

along this northbound causeway.

He is drawing new maps to the basket,

he is absorbing contact,

and he is brushing his shoulder off.

Everyone is taking note.

Even the scouts are smirking,

which is as close as they get to smiling.

(Golliver, page 121)

The Least Wrong Thing

Chris Spain

For my teachers

EMMIT DRIVES THE RENTAL NORTH FROM THE AIRPORT, RUNNING the heater hard, lost in beginnings, middles, this something that must be close to some end. He takes the interstate, skirts the foothills, drives an ancient uplift that after three hundred million years has been written down to plains by time. He has a hip ache from all the sitting, but he wants to get there before the day loses the last of its light.

Out the window is a country disappeared.

Disappeared because most of what he once knew is gone, and disappeared because, in this low winter light, anything other than close he can hardly see. Cataracts. Waterfalls of the eyes. As if he is looking through shattered glass. What he can see, what he remembers as pasture, barley stubble, center pivots, and turn rows, now, as near as he can tell, all houses.

A boyhood buried under houses.

He turns east off the highway, past what was once Langs, Tulps, Grants, and Trants. Then the dip at the slough, the slough already in a swale of shadow, and the right fender of the rental brushes up against what was once his family's farm. Before his mother and father died, before he sold the water rights and the land with it, before those people turned the place into a golf course. He doesn't even turn his head.

Another half mile and he'll be back to keep this hard promise.

When he and Kris were boys, hiking, climbing, any big adventure, they'd say, We're doing it Lewis and Clark, they'd say, We're doing it no maps.

Jesus, if ever, this is no maps.

The blue spruces throw him, the way they've grown, and he almost misses the turn. The big house is the same, with the same green and white trim. He parks half in milk barn shadow, half in light. The outlines of milk barn, pump house, tool shed, barn barn, help house, silo, corrals, all that still here; the old backboard too, but empty of rim and net.

Kris draining a jump shot, Emmit can almost see that. And Sonny tossing Emmit's red, white, and blue motorcycle helmet from the back porch, that hollow thunk when it hit the cement. But the elms are all stumps, and no Joe dog barks, and this close-in fence sags, foretelling the end of another farm.

Then Leigh is down the front porch steps and Emmit drops his rucksack.

She leans into him, her head into his shoulder, leaving him no place to put his arms but around her. That talc-like smell, that same smell of Leigh. And all the sandbagging in Emmit's heart washes away, just like that. How can this still happen? Her long hair still braided, she hasn't cut her hair. This must be one of the small gifts.

"You idiot," says Leigh. "Where's your jacket?"

The low distant hiss of the freeway.

The foothills turning their winter blue.

To have lived in the warmth of this woman.

Leigh opens the gas on a front burner, bends to look under the kettle for a flame. Emmit still feels her touch on his face, on his wrist, on the back of his hand. It's always been like this, from the first, every Leigh touch written into Emmit's skin for days.

The same blue carpet, the same blue love seat, the same old wood burning stove.

She wipes at her eyes, looks away again.

"I said I wasn't going to cry.

"You think you've cried every last tear and then, surprise."

Emmit, the best man, forty years ago, weeping in this same blue kitchen. After the service the preacher had come in to find him. It's a happy moment, the preacher said. I hope those are happy tears.

Out the big bay window the sweep of fields is halfway to becoming a 640-acre lake of dark. And just beyond, the surge of suburb lights. Emmit leans into the glass, as if that might help him see more.

"Looks like they got you pretty well surrounded."

The three of them stretched out on the hood of the old green Impala. That last summer, just before Emmit and Leigh get up to dance on the hood of the car, before Sonny starts yelling, before Sonny kicks Emmit off the farm. These are Emmit's own memory seeps; not leaking away, but leaking into the here and now, crowding this end of his life.

"How was the flight?"

The distant laugh-track babble of a television, on somewhere in the house. That's what he's been hearing.

"I think I'm still waiting for the plane to crash."

"I thought you got over that."

"I did," says Emmit. "For awhile."

As if he is standing on the thinnest tree limb, waiting for it to give. He doesn't really have a plan. Walking up the Dent is all he's got.

A closed in smell of urine, of body gone to fallow.

The same room that witnessed Alice waste away all those years, the glass in the windows replaced with what must be half-inch plywood, the sashes nailed shut. On the old cedar bureau are pictures of the farm when all around was still farms; of Sonny and Alice; of Emmit and Kris, on the front porch, with Leigh between them.

Kris is on a cot, watching the television, knees to his chest, rocking.

"Kris?" says Leigh.

He turns from the television, looks at Leigh, then looks at Emmit. Not a hint of recognition on his face, nothing at all. Emmit knows this is how it is, Kris's own sashes well nailed, but still.

"It's Emmit," says Leigh.

Kris pulls at the skin on his neck, looks from Leigh to Emmit, then back to Leigh.

"Who?"

"Emmit."

Emmit searches for traces, for any part of Kris that might be left. And then a hint of dawning recognition.

"Emmit?" says Kris, stumbling from the cot. "Emmit!"

He hugs Emmit hard. His mind mostly gone, but that farmer muscle still there.

"Goddamn it," says Kris. "I've been waiting. What took you so long? These damn people, they got me cooped up for ... for ... for Christ's sakes, thank God you're here. I thought you were never coming."

"It's good to see you, Kris."

His nails bitten down and the backs of his hands raw, red.

"This damn woman ... she's keeping me here, and we got hay to cut. There's no one cutting hay."

His voice is almost empty of what once made it his.

"It's winter, Kris," says Leigh. "There's no hay to cut."

"There's no hay? Well ... well hell! That's a fine fix you got us in. We'll have to slaughter the herd."

"We sold the cows," says Leigh, reaching to touch his shoulder.

"We did?"

"We got a good price."

Kris looks at her, then turns back to the television, seems to forget Emmit and the hay and the cows altogether. He scratches the backs of his hands, first one, then the other. Then he looks at Emmit again.

"You want to hear a joke?"

Emmit looks to Leigh, but she is staring at a boarded up window, as if she can still see what's beyond.

"Sure," says Emmit.

"So two cannibals are standing around this big steaming pot. Have you heard it?"

"No, I don't think."

"One says, I can't stand my mother-in-law. So the other, he says, If you can't stand her, just eat the noodles."

Emmit laughs for him.

"That's a good one," says Emmit.

But now Kris's smile is gone.

"I know why you're here," says Kris.

Emmit looks to Leigh, then back to Kris.

"You're here for the farm, aren't you? You're a fucking realtor."

"No," says Leigh. "It's Emmit."

Kris peers closer.

"Emmit!" says Kris, and he hugs Emmit like before.

The shutting down of the day has left them in a smaller space. Leigh hardly served herself, and even that, she's barely touched. But she's on her third glass of wine. Emmit imagines himself outside the bay window, looking in.

Two people, growing old together.

A taste of what he's missed in life, of a life not lived, like siphoning up a mouthful of gasoline.

"He's still his mother's son," says Leigh. "Mostly that gentleness hasn't left him. Even now. I've been lucky that way."

Emmit is sitting at this table, but he's also on a barn roof with Kris, almost beat to death by a summer of farming, but laughing. Laughing at the stupid cows. Laughing at nothing the way only best friends can laugh at nothing. They call each other their homemade epithets: You bottle cap–jumping volunteer fireman. You sock-sucking framer of the constitution.

And he's walking to that same barn, booting up swirls, walking to where Leigh waits for him. The first of the rain arriving, dust actually rising from the fall of the giant drops. She has gift wrapped herself in a lime green summer dress, the dress already falling off her shoulders. He doesn't know it then, but these will be his richest touches, never to be surpassed. Light spills through slat gaps in the warped and weathered wood. The pale triangles her swimming suit shades from the sun. The smell of that rain.

"I used to hate the television," says Leigh. "But it's the only thing that distracts him, keeps him from getting upset.

"He likes commercials best. I think because they're short enough for him to follow from beginning to end."

Emmit has stopped thinking in words, if he ever did. He is thinking in some other language, almost foreign, even to him, and it seems that by the time he gets it translated, it's too late, or the next day, or it just doesn't matter any more.

All they aren't talking about.

Carrying the firewood sling and a metal tray full of stove ashes, Emmit stumbles around outside in a graveyard of long dead days. Wearing Kris's boots and jacket, wrapped thick in the smell of Kris.

What is memory?

Just chemicals, a trick of chemicals, and Kris's chemistry gone bad.

Emmit rounds the milk barn, feels for the wind with the skin on his face, shifts his back to it, tips the tray. The ashes swirl and dance, float and disappear. Toward where Alice has been blowing around east of the cottonwoods it must be twenty years now.

The woodpile is almost as big as a mountain itself, practically stacked to the sky. Here is where the elms must be.

The smell of the animals, that's what's missing. That and Alice and Sonny and Emmit's own mother and father and Kris's mind and just about everything else.

Emmit knows his own big goodbye must be coming soon. It can't be that long. You just have to hope it happens like a tree falling on your head, fast as that, only time enough to see it blot the sky.

He lifts a hand, as if to feel for air still warm from when his boy self walked this same place. If he could write that boy a letter, what would he tell?

Nothing escapes the plow?

"You think you have enough firewood out there?"

Emmit sets the sling next to the stove, bends to slide the metal tray back.

"He likes to cut wood, he did," says Leigh.

Emmit crumples paper, builds a little kindling pyramid, lights it.

"I think he wanted to cut all I'd ever need. I mean he didn't say that, but that's what I think."

She pours them more wine.

"But then I kept finding him out on the road. Last summer made it all the way to the highway. So I had to stop letting him."

Emmit nearly misses the table with his glass, but catches it be it falls.

"You pretty much can't see, can you?"

"Only what I'm looking right at. If I don't look at it I can s

"A little bit Zen, I guess."

She doesn't ask, just drops his rucksack in her room, says sh even put sheets on the guestroom bed.

What looks to be a stack of thin books on her bedsid reading lamp. Glasses. Emmit is not sure where to put hin to be. He's still breathing from the stairs. He had to stop as if down to one lung. And he's planning on walking up

Then she's standing in the doorframe, silhouetted ag low hall light.

"He's asleep," says Leigh.

She turns off the hall light, crosses to Emmit.

"What's this?"

She touches his face.

"The dermatologist. She keeps cutting pieces of handsome off of me."

Leigh steps closer, hesitates for what seems a geologic age, kisses Emmit on the lips.

"Good thing you've still got a little bit to give."

He reaches for her hand.

His hand reaching for anything, for every glass of water, for the rock seam that saved his life; she was in all of that, all he ever reached for.

"As long as we haven't died yet," says Leigh. "And while I'm still a little drunk, I'm going to brush my teeth, take my clothes off, and get in this bed with you."

A wind chime startles.

Dead boys dodge from barn shadow to barn shadow, barefoot over diesel soaked dirt. A moon so bright it lights up the jet contrails like a giant tic-tac-toe.

"A giant tic-tac-toe," says Emmit.

Close his eyes, he's seventeen, he's a boy.

A touch in the barn is yesterday, is a lifetime ago. Reaching across those years to touch her face again. Her cheek, her chin, her lips.

Her hand reaching for his.

For most of his life, his life beyond repair, and now this.

"What am I to you, Emmit? Am I the worst thing that ever happened?"

"Worst and best."

"I didn't love you one more than the other, just that one of you needed me more.

"I think I thought that. Or knew it.

"Without thinking."

He finds himself at the west window, looking out.

How much later he's not sure.

High clouds, but still enough moon to throw shadows on the farm. The Front Range in distant silhouette, a vague darker dark against the sky. And out of the protection of the Dent, high on Witte Flats, at the bottom reaches of a glacial landscape, is a windswept frozen lake, waiting.

"Emmit?

"Emmit, what?"

"Is the Willis still running?"

A silence. He can't see her face.

"The last we checked. I checked."

"Do they still plow to French Meadows?"

She doesn't say.

"We don't have to," says Leigh. "It will be no different to him. He'll never know."

"I promised," says Emmit. "I gave him my word."

"It wasn't right of him to ask this of us," says Leigh. "To make us promise."

One of those quiets, until you can hear the house breathing.

"There may be no right thing. There may just be the least wrong thing."

Morning and Emmit finally gets himself out of bed and dressed. The night still with him, he's not letting go of that. Outside a dusting of snow, and a long east to west morning shadow of what looks to be the old orange Allis Chalmers, melting in its tracks.

Downstairs, at the front foyer door, old Kelty packs, down bags, snow shoes, a tent, a Primus stove, a blue canister of gas.

Kris is at the breakfast table, bits of toast scattered around him. Leigh has him shaved and showered, dressed in a red flannel shirt, heavy winter overalls, and a Front Range Seed cap. She's at the bay window, looking out.

Someone on the radio speaks of more flurries destined for the flatlands.

Leigh turns, almost smiles. Her face drawn and pale.

"There's coffee," she says.

She crosses to the counter, pours from a thermos, hands Emmit the cup. For the briefest moment her hand on his, the warmth of that. She fills her own cup, holds it close.

"There's still the small things," says Emmit. "There's still coffee."

When he looks at her, she doesn't look away. A moment caught and held.

"Am I late for class?" asks Kris.

They both turn to him.

"There's no class today," says Leigh.

"Oh," says Kris.

"What about the test?"

"No test, either," says Leigh.

Kris stares at Emmit.

"Hey, good morning," says Emmit. "It's Emmit."

But whatever Kris remembered yesterday, he's not remembering it now.

Leigh turns away from Emmit. She's facing the window again, looking out.

"If you're taking him up there, you have to go today. If you don't go today, I don't think I'm letting you."

Emmit looks at Leigh looking out the window.

He pulls out a chair, sits down next to Kris.

"Kris, you up for a camping trip?"

"Camping, I love camping!" says Kris. "When are we going camping?"

The old Willis, body metal rusted through in places, rains green paint on the world. Kris, looking expectant, looking excited, is already in the jeep, sitting in one of the cracked and split Camaro bucket seats they welded into the thing a lifetime ago.

"Huddle up, huddle up, first and ten," says Kris.

Emmit has already loaded the gear. He's at the tailgate, Leigh leaning into his shoulder. Her face still wet but she's stopped crying.

"It couldn't be just a regular god," says Leigh. "It would have to be some kind of evil genius god to think this up."

Emmit holds her, holds her tighter. Finally he steps back, hesitates, turns from her, gets in behind the wheel. She walks to the passenger side, reaches in through the window to touch Kris's face.

"It's the mountains, Kris," says Leigh, her voice faltering. "You love the mountains."

Her hand to his face again.

"I love you," Leigh says. "I loved you."

She leans into him, kisses him, then shakes her head, turns away.

"Go," she says, and she runs toward the house. "Go, go!"

When she reaches the front porch she hesitates, looks back, covers her face with her hands.

"She isn't coming?" asks Kris.

"No, no she's not."

Now the front porch empty.

"I like her . . . that girl," says Kris.

A foothill of the foothills.

Then the quick rise to the mouth of the canyon.

That familiar high-pitched whine of the three speed, the air tinged with exhaust. A haze of floorboard dirt, or maybe it's just Emmit's eyes. He tries to read the road signs by not looking at them, and this one he finally makes out: The Pass is closed until Memorial Day.

Along the river he can make out trees, but not what they are; mountain ash, scrub oak, must be. Down here there isn't much snow, just on the north side of things, under overhangs. And then he steers them into the shadows of The Fall.

"The Fall," says Emmit.

As if this road, these curves and banks, these steeps and drops, are imprinted on some part of his soul.

"You remember riding this on our inner tubes, in summer?" asks Emmit.

Kris is rocking again.

"Your mom driving us up here, towels stuffed in our cutoffs, to save us busting our asses. That one time coming around a big boulder and those two college girls changing, buck naked, and us hooting and hollering?"

Kris smiles.

"You remember?"

"You want to hear a joke?" says Kris. "There's these two cannibals standing around a big steaming pot. Have you heard it?"

"Yes," says Emmit. "I have."

"You have?"

"The one says, If you can't stand her, just eat the noodles."

Kris's face falls in on itself. And tears, real tears.

"Oh, Jesus," says Emmit.

But looking over, and looking again, he sees the moment leave Kris, watches his expression change from hurt, to confused, to almost serene.

Kris wipes at his eyes, and the tears are completely gone.

The confluence of The Fall and The Little Fall, then that narrowing at Deep Cut. Wine-colored cliffs and Little Fall lashed boulders. Emmit considers what looks to be an unprotected drop, and he can almost see the Willis going over the edge of it. That would be a tree on your head.

But then, quick as that, they are out of canyon shadow and into the gleaming opening up of French Meadows. The sun reflects off the snow and it's as if they have driven up on some giant arc-welder. Emmit slows, slows some more. Waiting for resolution, waiting for the hard lines to fall back into place. Until he sees the Dent, and the looming Teachers.

He parks at the curve in the road, where the plow swings wide to make the turn before heading back down the canyon. He hurries their gear out, to get started before some ranger or plow driver shows up to ask what these two old guys are doing up here in winter. Kris has gotten himself out of the passenger side and turns slow circles.

"This is a lot of white," says Kris.

"The far end of French Meadows," says Emmit. "We're going camping."

"We're going camping?" says Kris. "I love camping! When are we going camping?"

"Now, we're going right now."

Kris has stopped turning. He stares up the Dent.

"You remember the Dent?" asks Emmit.

Kris doesn't say but keeps staring.

"We have to get these snow shoes on you."

"Snow shoes?" says Kris. "Do I know snow shoes?"

"Sure you do, these are yours."

Emmit gets a pair of gloves on Kris, drops his own, fumbles to get Kris's boots into the bindings.

"You have to stay still."

Even in the sun this high altitude cold is insistent, with an edge on it, and Emmit's fingers quickly numb.

No sound from Shader Creek.

It's frozen, without a trickle. But the trail is marked with white blazes every few trees and looks mostly clear. Douglas fir, must be, these planks of shadow. The skin on Emmit's face recalls the touch of this light, exactly. This was the entrance to their temple, their holy place.

"Where does this go?" asks Kris.

"Up the Dent. To McKiernan's Lake, to the Divide."

"To the Divide," says Kris.

He steps past Emmit, starts up the trail.

"Where you going?"

"I think I know the way," Kris says.

"Great," says Emmit. "Pace yourself."

Kris doesn't even look back. A stone, dislodged by Kris, tumbles across the snow pack, clatters to the frozen Shader.

To rest there a thousand years, just the same as that.

"Follow the white blazes!" calls out Emmit.

Metamorphic gneiss and schist eroded down to jagged crags.

Emmit turns the word over. Metamorphosis. From all this rich-ness to a scattering of ash, a handful of loess. A handful of loss.

But the Shader, the Dent, and these mountains, this sky, they will remain. There should be some comfort in that.

Kris has disappeared, swallowed by rock, snow, and tree.

And here his blue jacket.

"Kris!" shouts Emmit.

The breath cloud drifts in front of his face, dissipates.

Little teaspoons of air, that's all Emmit's getting.

Just these sips.

Thighs cramping. Snow shoes dragging. Blood clanging in his ears. He reaches a grove of Aspen, empty of leaves. These naked trunks could be white leg bones stripped of sinew and muscle.

And then he is here but not here.

It's late summer, not winter, and they've reached the lake before realizing they forgot the beer, and they do rock, paper, scissors, or something, and Emmit loses, so he has to hike down to the jeep, to get the forgotten beer, and on the way back up, when he reaches these trees, these same trees, the sun is almost buried in the Divide, and it's as if the light is coming from the insides of the yellow quaking leaves, and even though Leigh has already happened, even though every-thing is already fucked up and always will be, even though Emmit has never loved anyone the way he loves Leigh, he has never loved anyone the way he loves Kris, either, and he stands in the shimmering yellow middle of it, thinking, if he built a heaven, this is what it would look like, with him walking up the Dent, with the forgotten beer, to Kris, who's building a fire, staking their tent.

"Kris!"

Wind timber down everywhere, tripping Emmit when he forgets.

He finally finds Kris on a rock outcropping, lost in a view of the Teachers. Some kind of catastrophe is happening in Emmit's chest.

This could solve everything. He'll just drop dead of a heart attack and Kris will hike off the top of a mountain.

"Jesus," says Emmit, still hunting for air. "What . . . what have you been doing? Training for a marathon?"

Kris turns to Emmit.

"What?" says Emmit.

"I can't remember the number," says Kris.

"What number?"

"I'm lost, I don't know where I am."

"You're not lost, you're with me. You're with Emmit. We're walking up the Dent, to Witte Flats, to McKiernan's Lake."

Kris doesn't look convinced.

"I know you, don't I? How else would I know your name?" asks Emmitt

"I know you?"

"It's Emmit, goddamn it, your best friend."

"Emmit?"

"This here, this scar on your forehead, that was from us playing hoe-throw. I whacked you right there"

Kris reaches to touch where Emmit just touched him.

"You hit me?"

"By accident, I wasn't looking, neither of us was. My mom was not happy."

Kris still touches his forehead. Now he stares at Emmit, as if he might really be seeing him.

"Emmit?"

"I got older," says Emmit.

"You sure did."

Out of the protection of the Dent, high on Witte Flats.

The last of the trees, stunted, stagger the slopes of the Teachers. It's a whitewashed world of snow and ice, and with nothing to stop the wind, it's as if the jet stream reaches right down to the ground.

This is a future with some teeth in it, with some knives.

And Emmit's sweat freezing. And the snow deep and drifted. And Kris already leaving him behind.

Kris has remembered something because he's dropped his pack under the lonely limber pine, the same tree they always hung their food bags from. He stands close, at the edge of the frozen lake, peering out over it. Emmit lets his own pack slide from his back, leans his forehead into the tree.

"Made it," gasps Emmit.

His brain already a little bit frozen. He can hardly think, he can't think.

This is where his plan ends.

"You remembered," says Emmit. "You remembered our camp."

"Where is . . . where is the woman?"

Emmit still working to get his lungs back.

"Leigh?

"She's at the farm."

"She's . . . she's not coming?"

"No, no she's not."

"Is she okay?"

"She's okay."

The wind stronger and Kris hunches over, his arms crossed in front of his chest, holding his shoulders close. The discarded blue jacket is in Emmit's pack, but he's not giving it back. Unless Kris asks. Probably not even then.

"Shouldn't . . . shouldn't . . . shouldn't we go inside?" asks Kris.

"There is no inside."

"Oh."

Kris turns another slow circle, takes in the high peaks of the Teachers to the west, the wide flat of the frozen lake, the clouds piling over the Divide, the faltering light.

"Is this the top of the world looking down?"

"Almost."

"Are we lost?"

"This is McKiernan's Lake, up at the Divide, practically our home."

But the worry doesn't leave Kris's face.

"What are we talking about here?" asks Kris.

"What are we talking about?"

Kris jerks his head around, looking over his shoulder, as if he is afraid something might be sneaking up behind him. And Emmit is sure that, somewhere, maybe in that place beyond language, Kris understands.

"I have a bad feeling," says Kris.

He backs away from Emmit, out on to the frozen lake.

With the sun gone the temperature drops almost violently, falling twenty, maybe thirty degrees. Snow ticks off Emmit's hood, as if time made visible.

No, not visible, he is hearing it.

Kris is out on the ice, in his overalls and red flannel, swaying back and forth, a dim and distant flame. Now the snow heavier and soon Kris will disappear altogether.

Emmit gets himself standing.

The lake is solid of course, like walking concrete. The ice wiped clean, polished by this wind. As if from above, as if through some god's eye, Emmit watches this feeble attempt at . . . what?

"I need to talk to you," says Emmit.

A wind gust.

The earth trying to flee this moment, rushing away through space.

"I can't, I can't feel my . . . these," says Kris.

He's lost his gloves.

"Hands," says Emmit.

"Hands?"

Curtains of snow move toward them. Drifting veils.

"I want you to work hard to remember this, Kris. We grew up together. I'm your best friend, I lived two farms over. My dad was Jay, you remember them? Jay and Jane?"

"Jay and Jane," says Kris.

"We were best friends, for a long time. And then Leigh came, the girl, the woman from the farm, and we both fell in love with her. You remember that? And then she chose you.

"This is important, Kris. When your mom died, when I came back and we scattered your mother's ashes, you told me if you ever got as bad as that, as your mother, your mother Alice, you made me swear I'd take you up here in winter, walk you up the Dent, to the Divide.

"Do you remember that?

"You said what happened to your mother was like being chewed to death by the dull teeth of a grazer. You said, Take me up there in winter, then tell me you forgot the beer, and leave me.

"You made me promise, you made me give you my word."

As if Kris really is working to remember.

"We forgot the beer?"

"No," says Emmit. "No, that was from before.

"It's what I'm going to do. I'm going to let you freeze to death.

"If that's what you still want."

Kris's teeth chattering.

"Well . . . well . . . did you pinky swear? That's . . . what counts. If you didn't pinky swear, they can't prove anything."

The Primus long dead.

Snow gone, wind gone, now just this seeping cold. Past moon set, but up this high, light from the stars enough to see with.

All that wealth, dwindled down to this.

As if Emmit is in the jaws of something himself, the cold locking him down.

Kris is bent over his knees.

"If . . . if . . . if you give a party, and no one comes, that's the worst thing."

"You gave a party and no one came?" asks Emmit.

"This party, I'm saying this party."

Kris tries to stand, but already it is beyond him.

"But I didn't study."

"You didn't study for what?"

"For . . . for the test."

"The test is over.

"You made perfect."

"I made perfect?"

"You got the highest score."

"Oh."

Now Kris breathing harder, as if he is on some unconquerable slope.

"This might be the biggest adventure," says Emmit.

"Lewis and Clark, you remember? No maps.

"Pay attention, okay?"

"Okay," says Kris. "Okay, but . . . there isn't much hot."

These the last words Kris speaks.

How much time passes, Emmit doesn't even know.

Enough time.

Kris doesn't sag, he doesn't fall over, just that he is breathing, and then he isn't.

Emmit waits to be sure, holding his breath himself.

Yes, he has kept his hard promise.

He looks up at the void, at the swallowing vault, his eyes blurring.

He works a glove off, touches two fingers to his lips, then to Kris's lips, says a prayer, to the god he doesn't believe in.

Okay.

He has walked Kris right to the door, and seen him through it.

Okay. Now he has to get that glove back on.

He has to get that glove on and the tent up and in a warm bag or no one is walking out of here. First the glove, then the tent.

That's a good plan.

But what if this is as happy as an ending gets?

What if he is right where he wants to be? High in the Teachers, up at the Divide, his favorite place on earth, with his dead best friend.

"I wonder if this is as happy as an ending gets?"

Emmit says this to himself and his dead best friend.

He wishes Leigh were here to ask. If Leigh were here he could ask her.

He isn't cold anymore, he's almost warm.

That's not good.

Emmit knows he's dying if he doesn't get that tent out of his pack. He's dying if he doesn't stand right now and shake those poles and stakes out of the bag and get some protection up.

But he really doesn't know what he is going to do.

What's the right thing.

To either leave Kris off here alone, or walk with him through.

That last long horizontal light of summer spills over the Front Range. The summer they are fifteen. Before Sonny throws Emmit off the farm, before Emmit starts working summers in Texas, before his mother and father die, before Emmit sells the water and the land with it.

The last summer before Leigh.

Emmit and Kris ride a blue mini-bike stripped of muffler and governor, blasting between the barley and the beans. They are still trying on their new bodies, their almost-a-man bodies, and life is all promise and they will never be richer. One of them drives. The other is on back, holding on with just knees, aiming a .22 rifle at this Olympic jackrabbit that is out-running them in the turnrow. Whoops and shouts.

They don't see where the irrigation ditch has broken until they are on the mud slick and the mini-bike spins, flips, dumps them hard, the one with the rifle holding it high, so as not to shoot either of them.

The blue mini-bike drowns an ugly death in the irrigation ditch. The jack rabbit is well escaped, got away, living for another day.

They look at each other.

Mud smeared. A little blood smeared.

They are alive.

They throw their heads back and laugh and laugh.

Midnight

William Benton

You can see the sea
smeared with shimmer,

palms chatter in the year
I mean the yard. I'm

a little bit nervous
visited by a presence

of cessation, drinking
beer on the screened-in

porch, the wild shore
the one girl all

that self is
and then is not.

The Tin Room

At dinner she makes
an accomplice. Cackles

and peeks from behind
the bones of her fingers.

Filaments of web
settle weightlessly

into place. A
scrim of smoke

follows the motion
of her hand. Silent,

divided against ourselves
we leave the restaurant

baffled by the infallible
performance

that requires now
with her walking

up the street
our pity.

William Benton

Saltwater

The light moves like
nerves on the water

white jittery lines
I can see the shadow of
my head its own

dark confusions.

Palms shift in the wind.
We were all silent,

the children aware,
an incalculable

weight, their arms
thin as flutes.

I'm sorry; I can't stay.

She steps onto
the veranda,

beacon, flower,

outlined against
yellow squares

of lattice-work
and the sea beyond

beyond Bonnard.

Science

For Nat

Arranged in a single
cluster, tiny insects

with coral colored wings
mimick a flower.

We know this because
they survived.

Two things happened   they lived
and at the same time

revealed the veil
of destiny reversed.

They lived like love,
beyond disaster,

in a form entirely
its own proof. Otherwise

all we'd know of them
is mute absence —

nothing—
another branch.

But what I'm left with at the end
is no different to what I had when I
began: a set of keys, a "conversation."
A gift.

(Gunn, page 21)

A King in Mirrors

Matthew Specktor

The New Soft Shoe

MY FATHER TOSSES ME INTO THE AIR. I HAVE NO IDEA WHEN, OR if, I will come down. My face splays out like a race car driver's, pinned back against my skull. I feel my bones, my stomach, my heart, my kidneys—all things I have seen pictured in a book—sliding around inside their loose cage of skin. When he's finished, and all of my worst fears have been shown but not proven, he hands me to my uncle.

"Here." He is doughy, soft and huge like a walrus. He walks away, laughing.

Such is my introduction to my body. Inside my room, I practice with it. What does it do? I put on side two of *The White Album* and spasm uncontrollably to "Helter Skelter," to "Everybody's Got Something to Hide." Every day is my birthday, until my uncle—a joyless hardass, who lives alone in Mar Vista—asks me what I'm doing.

"Dancing."

"That's not dancing," he snaps. He shows me instead what might be, moving around the room in a sequence of elaborate steps that seem chalked across the floor, diagrammed in white. He hums under his breath, "Moon River," and for a moment we are in the South Pacific, on one of the nameless atolls that decorate the globe over in the corner. Palms sway outside my window. My uncle is lost too, I think, in whatever world of Waves and Wacs, scarlet fever and diphtheria—I am aware my parents grow backwards, into a world that predates the polio vaccine and the Beatles—he came from. Eventually, he loses interest, drops my hands and brushes me off his feet. My poor uncle, who never married and has no kids of his own. Sadness ticks off him, there in the corner, as he stands with his hands on his knees. The needle hisses in the run-out groove. Behind the house they are digging a hole in the yard. I listen to the men shouting, the bulldozer's solemn rumble. My uncle straightens and walks from the room. He has a finely fuzzed head, soft like a peach, and he smells like hot skin, cleaning fluid: some sweet, decaying smell I can't name. I try to imagine what he was like when he was funny. When, for instance, he very elaborately switched out the family's cream of wheat with wood shavings, so his father sat down—this would've been in March of 1939, when my mother was seven and he fourteen—to a hot bowl of sawdust. I picture this perfectly: the stern savage who is supposed to look like me, pouring himself some orange juice, and then whipsawing suddenly, keeling forward to hit the table face first. For a long moment, no one speaks. My mother's family are all absurdists, deadpan practitioners of jokes that aren't funny. Orange juice dribbles over the side of the table and Spencer, the dog, laps it up. Nails scrabbling atop linoleum. Finally someone laughs and my mother reaches over and pokes her dad's clammy, inert skin.

All this has been explained to me, with talk of a *congenital defect*, a *closed valve*, but I think it's the most terrifying thing I've heard in my life. It finds its mirror in the racket the Beatles are now making, a clatter of found sounds and restaurant scrapings—*number 9, number 9*—I'll never listen to again. Outside, the men keep shouting, the bulldozer digs its hole. Eventually this will be a swimming pool. For now it's a grave, a pit I climb in and out of at will, rehearsing my own retirement. The record, the shouting, the nightmare grind. These things blur, they run together: my grandfather, born with a bad heart, and the hours, the world, the ordinary clamor of the day.

Flaming

My parents take me to see a psychiatrist. A boy I know has just died hang-gliding.

"Why are you afraid?"

I don't have an answer. His office looks like an abstract painting, grid-like and disorderly. He is a set of glasses concealing, somewhere far behind him, a man. Bald like my uncle, my grandfather, like me someday. *A maternal gene.*

"Are you afraid of other things? Besides dying?"

I am afraid of light fixtures, uncooked hot dogs, chicken livers; I am afraid of the bright blue gizzard I've seen in a disemboweled rattlesnake, a scream that is emitted on the second side of the *Hair* soundtrack. I am afraid of my own heart. My mother stands in the kitchen on one foot, talking on the phone while she burns sandwiches.

"Oh that's awful," she says, tapping her cigarette against the edge of the counter. Her frail, pale face like the lady on the Yuban can, framed by platinum strands. "How did it happen?"

Flakes drift down toward the floor, gray snow. My sandwich when she hands it to me is black, carbonized, the cheese almost liquid. I like it like that, eat it cheerfully while I listen to the gardener attack the grass outside. I can't help but notice however that people are dying, that men are marching on the moon. I eat and feel weightless, uncertain. I walk up to the television while Marlon Perkins is talking. "I know him," I proclaim, hands against the glass, as if I might tumble through it to Africa.

"No you don't," my mother says. "Sorry honey, but you don't."

Sunday evening, I'll be asleep by 7:30, the living room rug the same color as the Serengeti. While I sleep, perhaps, a friend of my mother's is killed in a shootout with the police. Another, a colleague of my father's, commits suicide in his garage. *Monoxide, closet, Black Panther.* The words are suggestive, but don't make sense.

"Did Sheila know?" my mother asks. While I sit on the floor and strike blue-tipped kitchen matches against ribbed glass; sniff the inside of a cedar-lined box, like a silver coffin. "How could she not know, he was flaming?"

I could ask, but I don't. It's more interesting not to know, to say nothing of safer. *What's gunrunning, who are pigs, why is Roman Polanski crying?* My parents barricade their doors against things that haven't happened yet. In their room, and through the door, my mother speaks the word "leukemia." I hear my father say, "That's too bad, Ren, that's too bad."

At Roxbury Park, a little girl I've been playing with—her name is Mariana Dopp—stops coming. My mother sits with the profile of a statue, while I tumble alone below the trees. *Dopp, rhymes with stop.* These things make a crooked, associative pattern, spinning out around death. I look up at the moon, pale and vaporous in the afternoon sky. A eucalyptus rains sticky pods on my palms. *Why is she bald, mom, why is she bald?* Later in the evening my parents throw a dinner party. I listen to them, from bed, the voices drifting up the stairs. I'm not in the least sleepy. I take three curtain calls, steal slices of prosciutto—tattered, disintegrating like dried skin—off slices of greening melon. When I am out of excuses, I go back upstairs. Their voices are garbled, faraway, like passengers' on a ship. They are singing, singing "Auld Lang Syne." I am wide awake. Over the hedge the neighbors are awake too, every light in their house blazing. I lie perfectly still. A chandelier hangs above me like a bomb. The singing collapses at last into laughter, my mother's voice riding drunkenly above the rest. *Goodnight, goodnight.* My eyes stay locked upon the window next door, counting the seconds, the minutes, the hours, just waiting for the light to go out.

The Good Doctor

"Let's go to Martindales," my father says. "Let's go to Beverly Hills."

It's Saturday morning, the day spreads endlessly before us. His friend, The Good Doctor, picks us up in a Grand Am. He's not a doctor he's an actor, an Englishman: I've seen him on TV, scrutinizing viruses through a microscope, playing a scientist striving to save the world. He smells sweet and vaguely urinous. He is handsome, in just the way his nickname implies: leathery, box-jawed, hair flecked with early silver. I am older, I can read a menu, my mother has given me a copy of *Tom Sawyer* that will obsess me for the next year-and-a-half. In the darkness of the Hamlet on Century Park East—a room like a casket, velveteen and windowless—we eat our Rex Harrisons, the Number 9 with Russian dressing, the waitresses fail to recognize The Good Doctor. What could be wrong with them? *I'm fine, thank you and you*, my father says to everyone who greets him and I wonder who the ghost is, the invisible second to whom my father is also speaking?

Outside, there are pyramidal steps, a shape like a ziggurat that I wind my way around, trying to keep my balance while my dad and The Good Doctor discuss business.

"They're squeezing our balls," my father says, "but I'm going to get you what you deserve. We'll take you to another network if we have to."

"Those bastards." For a moment, they forget I am here. "I can't afford not to get picked up, you know that don't you?"

The Good Doctor holds my hand so I don't fall. What would I do without him? A Ferris wheel lifts into the air, in the distance. The Good Doctor looks that way too. His wife, Peggy, is having tests run at Cedars of Lebanon. Something is not right, a problem with her ovaries. Neither of these men, wise grown-ups, is yet forty years old. The air is the color of ash, there where the Ferris wheel touches it, beyond the tops of the conifers that mark the edge of a golf course. He lets go my hand a moment, reaches up to adjust his glasses. My father sits, his chinless face—he looks like a Hell's Angel gone tender, gone soft—trained upon the ground. Maybe he's counting the bricks, which I do too: the pinkish rectangular tiles that line the restaurant's courtyard. His own father is in the same hospital, coughing up his lungs. Later, we go visit him, just the two of us now. We stand in the hospital elevator, on our way to see a person neither of us understands, his accent thickening under so much phlegm I can barely decipher a word of it. I rub the Braille plate, next to the regular buttons, as we lurch skywards. I look at my copy of Tom Sawyer, so full of things I don't understand either—what is "ambuscade," what are Arabs, what are bulrushes?—yet I don't care. I vanish inside the sounds.

Shadow Dancing

My father throws away his cigarettes, takes up running.

"Come on," he says. It's six o'clock in the morning. "Come on."

We're living in Santa Monica now, home of the newlywed and the nearly dead, my mother calls it. It's 1977. The pier, the mall, the promenade are all derelict, and crumbling towers crouch at the base of Ocean Avenue, their balconies pendular with dead ferns. There's no one awake at this hour. The sky is gray, a plain dull mother of pearl. We run to the ocean and back. I wake up, warm into hating my father the way I do. Every step hurts, feels concussive and unnatural even in my soft shoes. I wear headphones, a transistor radio tuned to an AM station plays Andy Gibb. The day cracks open like an egg as we jog along Ocean, and yet there's nobody here. The wide streets, the brass balustrades of the Shangri-La Hotel and the Bellevue, places where the retirees cluster to eat Crab Louis at twilight. We go home and I dress for school, while my father lines up his vitamins and chokes them down, two by two. He's shaved his face in an effort to look younger. I still recognize him, but it's possible my mother doesn't. The Zegna ties, the manicures, the spritzers. Up in my room, Suzie—the dog I've had since I was two—lies perfectly still beneath the windowsill. Her side rises and falls, rises and falls, her gray fur mottles with the carpet. She is blind in one eye, limping, she smells like wet feathers, like slow rot. Soon she will fall into the swimming pool and drown. "Hello?"

The voice on the other end of the phone is garbled, gross with its own weight and importance when I pick up on Saturday afternoon. I call my dad and pretend to hang up, though of course, of course, I listen.

"Freddy, Freddy, I've got to get off this picture—

"I can't get you off of it. It's a contract. It'll be a horse's head in *your* bed, next time—

I crouch in the den, barely daring to breathe. I've seen the movie, blood streaking the producer's silk sheets. There might be marbles in the man's mouth, coins on his eyes. How can he talk this way?

"Freddy, Freddy, what can you do?"

Over my bed, in my room, there is a poster that summarizes female beauty. A woman with ringlets, raccoon eyes, a maroon tube top. This image is everywhere—in three years, it'll be antique—but now it's in everyone's room, all around the world. I come home to find her standing inside the vestibule, talking to my mom about shoes. She looks like her own quotation, like an echo of something that didn't exist before she invented it. I yawn, plod upstairs. When your fantasies belong to everybody they cease to be interesting, cease to be yours. Maybe, instead, they cease to be credible. Yet—the signs are everywhere. Why can't I read them? Every morning the boulevards are crowded now with men like lemmings, stampeding to the sea and back. My father and I are no longer alone. Their greasy torsos and hollow eyes, their stallion bodies as they run, breathing violently, pivoting upon the Pacific's coolness and back, back to their ranch-style bungalows and unhappy children, their jilted wives softening beneath the kiwi trees. Or else to their condominiums in Brentwood, the empty two bedrooms let furnished, rooms and refrigerators bare except for crushed boxes of Monopoly and Scrabble, half-bottles of Soave Bolla and rancid hacks of salmon. At one of these, belonging to a friend's father, I find a dildo underneath a couch. When A___'s dad is murdered, it seems almost a relief to the rest of us. We waste our time acting it out, garroting one another or stabbing, leaving fist-sized bruises on one another's skinny chests.

That this life, with its dream of infinite extension—I've heard my father, too, use the word *cunt*—should end just like any other.

Bone, or Cream

"Till death! You said, 'Till death!'"

My parents are fighting downstairs, my mom's voice hysterical. I lie in bed and listen, try to find some other explanation beyond the obvious. I hold my breath, my tongue tastes of hashish. "Moonage Daydream" blares through headphones, but I can hear everything: the ice rattling in my mother's glass, her voice more animal than human.

"Who is she?" she shouts. "What's her name?"

I am beginning to feel doomed to unoriginality, beginning to suspect an adult life is more wearisome than a child's. Like it or not, I am a conscript in true love's army. At this hour, certain songs mean everything to me. "City of the Dead." "Watching the Detectives." When my father leaves, I shake his hand and watch him walk off, tramping across the shabby grass. That's his car, parked at the curb, a Mercedes I've never seen before. It's white, and sinister in the moonlight. Its ragtop is rolled back in the rain.

"What's her name?"

My mother asks me now, plaintively this time, and I shrug. I know, but I can't tell her. She knows, but pretends not to. Their marriage lasted seventeen years and suddenly—she confides in me—he changed everything it is possible to change, everything outside his own skeleton. I realize—as my mother uncorks a second bottle of wine for the two of us—that this has been bothering me—my father's new car is not white, but "bone," or "cream." Or both. Can it be both? It doesn't matter, he has a new one—newer still—when he shows up to visit, when he spends the night in a moment of deep contrition and then bails again, leaving behind a tan Members Only jacket, several sizes too small. My mother weeps and weeps and weeps. Her cheek is flush with the butcher's block table in the kitchen, where she is asleep or unconscious, I can't tell. Her nightgown hangs open. I pass by, ignoring her, ignoring the sight of my mother's tits. Up in my room, I play David Bowie, the one about the Thin White Duke, "throwing darts in lovers' eyes." What I, after all, would like to do. It's late, I'm awake, and somewhere outside my father's Porsche roars throatily along the avenues, the ghostly sound of the automotive suburbs. I pour myself another shot, draw one more line. My face is numb, my teeth like a beaver's, hard enough to chip wood. My father is out there, leading his obscure and elegant life. Mine might last longer, but only—I lift my face from the mirror and close my eyes—only if I'd like.

Rehearsal

My father collapses at The Palm. He takes a bite of his dessert and then turns blue, swooning across the table, leaving skidmarks of chocolate mousse on white cloth.

"Oh my God!" my stepmother yells, more convincingly than she ever has on screen. "Oh my God!"

For a moment, no one notices. Her voice sounds off the walls and marbles with the gossip, the murmur of all the other diners, the pictures of Lew Wasserman and Tony Perkins, Don Rickles and Harry Cohn.

"Oh my God!" she screams again. And people look up from their piles of shoestring potatoes finally, those towers that look like tiny kindling. A waiter runs and wraps his arm around my father's waist, squeezes. Maybe she is less convincing than I thought for I don't, even while this is happening, believe her. Around the room faces are raised from plates of scallops, skin tones red and gold, to look at my father writhing and choking, before he coughs up whatever was blocking his windpipe. A bit of cake, so they can go back to eating their own.

No story here. Nothing has happened. My stepmother touches her hair, that rat's nest of brittle darkness, and forks ring out against china. My father drinks a glass of water. When John Belushi died, Leigh Brillstein showed me her true face, which was everyone's true face, streaked with tears. She sat beneath the halogen tubes, the hum of electric typewriters and telex machines around her, while she hung up the phone quietly. When the news was announced, three hours later, Leigh was already in crisis mode, regal as a queen while she fielded condolence calls, leaving it to the media to weep and moan. Had my father died, this would've been my job. No one here would do it sooner. I am twenty-two, a paperback *Hamlet* jammed deep within my pocket, a college diploma—still bleeding ink—rolled up in the backseat of my car. People resume eating, their faces placid as cows. *No one we know, anyway.* Around them, around us all, the caricatures on the walls bound up like superheroes, gigantic heads attached to cricket bodies. Don Rickles to the rescue! Please tell me how to live, what to do.

Allergies

D___ goes to London. Theater is his life. He sends me a Dadaist postcard decorated with stick figures, a long, long letter detailing everything—the conversion rates, the coldwater flat in Hampstead, the view from the buses along Charing Cross Road, the man whose nose is half his face—until I am jealous. I yearn to be him. The pages of the letter are dusted with hair, he writes: *I am allergic to everything, I can't stop sneezing, this flat smells funky.* It belongs to a poet, an older man who has gone abroad. *These fucking cats!* What does it matter? He is living a dream. In high school we wore long coats and ate peyote, staggering around the campus after dark. We broke into the science building, chased each other down the long, dark halls, banging fiercely against the empty lockers. *Are you scared yet,* we'd yell. *Are you scared yet??* Not yet, not ever. If they couldn't catch us now, how were they supposed to do so in the future? Flashlights under our faces, skin dripping off our bones. In London he lives on porridge and orange juice, a healthy lifestyle. We've moved on. *But why does this place reek so*, he asks in a letter that reaches me at a temp desk in San Francisco, where I am adjudicating a suit between Mastercard and Visa, typing and retyping nearly identical forms. *Fruitless, fruitless.* I really ought to be in London, instead of temping for the man, dying (I suspect, and it feels like) by inches. I write back, in Liquid Paper. *S.O.S! Some Pig! Help Me Please!* Soft, calligraphic brushstrokes, on blue stationary. I wait and I wait. I get no response. On the phone with my mother, one day she says, "Honey, I'm sorry to tell you but that boy in your class? The one who won a Fulbright? He died."

"Died?"

Yes, died. The explanation tumbles out in a rush, something about a gas leak, a few beers, a headache, a nap. He never woke up. I sit at my desk staring out at the Transamerica Pyramid, Coit Tower at twilight, ruins of a civilization that hasn't collapsed yet as my mother—suddenly sober, shuttling herself from meeting to meeting—apologizes. For what, I wonder? Because I am young, I think too, never sorry enough.

I quit my job. But not before I get one last letter, which comes as I'm cleaning out my desk. I open the airmail envelope and find—a ziplock baggie full of mold? Are they spores, toxic, a new drug? They look like an old man's pubes, gray-green, something scraped off a peach: only when I find the note do I understand.

I shaved the cat, he has written. The solution! *I shaved the cat!*

The Stupidest Movie in the World

This is how it goes, for a while. We have entered the new territory. We have found our feet, it appears. For example G___, last seen scavenging in a Dumpster behind the Santa Monica Promenade, reinvents himself as a successful stockbroker. He shows up gleaming, in a new suit, his red hair and freckles still screaming Trust Me!, the needle marks invisible along his arms. Wonderful, we want to applaud! Bravo! I knew you'd make it, I almost tell him, but don't. So-and-so directs the Stupidest Movie of All Time, then laughs his way to the bank. We attend the premiere, applaud with enthusiasm. The movie is so bad we can enjoy it without feeling envious of his model girlfriend, the pimpwear he sports—irony, irony—as he glides across the lobby of the DGA. There he goes! Waiting to embrace him, why—it's The Good Doctor! He's in the movie too, but who isn't? His turn as an animal rights activist who gets mixed up with the mob is an homage or a parody, whereas our own—my own, performance as myself—is what, precisely? I go over to say hello to him. He squints at me like an assailant. *Oh,* he says. *Yes, I remember. How's your father?* I tell him, and think: maybe I am the second self, the one my father was always talking to. He pats my shoulder and then walks away to join a woman I don't recognize. Peggy is dead, their own children both grown, both suicides.

We keep on, though. We just keep getting away with it. Until P___'s sister dies of an aneurysm, collapsing on the floor of her terrace in Westwood, peach-colored nightgown bunched around her ankles, textbooks scattered around her head. Until X___'s mother gets bone cancer, and some kid we barely remember succumbs to kidney failure, then has a building named after him. Memorial services are held on the Paramount lot. Respectfully, we attend. I preen agelessly in a restroom outside the theater, a white chrysanthemum in the buttonhole of my blue jacket. Unless—wait! That's at my wedding. I am there, to my own amazement as well as anybody's. *Remember that night you crashed behind the ice machine, wearing argyle socks?* I do not. I hardly remember anything, although the words, spoken below the clustering thunderheads, are as present as can be. *I will,* I say, looking over my wife's shoulder at the cemetery, where the stones are all eroded beyond legibility, all covered with a radiant green moss. Should I attribute to any of this a special significance? To the clouds rolling in over the bay? Of course I shouldn't, of course I don't. I take a drink from a passing waiter and watch these—soft pink, edged with lemon peel—drifting across the lawn, shimmering in the dark like fireflies. There go my parents, on speaking terms! And here comes my bride, inexplicable in her dress, like a column of melting foam or like everything I have neglected to ask for in my entire life.

God's Eye

I wake up screaming. It happens naturally. There's a crick in my neck, my knees don't work the way they used to. My wife leaves, almost before she was ever here. I wake up, lifting my face off the pillow that is wet, and has muffled my animal groan. *Are you a camel*, my daughter says? *Daddy, are you a giraffe?*

"Something like it," I said, turning my face away. She shouldn't see me like this, I shouldn't see me like this. "I'm a primate."

"What's a primate?" she says.

"A primate's a monkey. Just like—you!"

I leap from bed and attack her, giggling. She hiccups with laughter. I won't let her stop. Sunlight lops off the bottoms of the palms, plantains dangled past my window. Does anything ever change, besides everything? Besides the need for colonoscopies and the meaning of the shopping list—not my writing still taped to the fridge? I have no idea, and yet the same sad Santas go drooping across Wilshire Boulevard, the same gay tinsel marks the gateway to Beverly Hills. My daughter oohs and aahs at the same fountain—the one my father once peed in after a function at the Hilton—on the corner of Sawtelle and Sepulveda. Only there is no such corner, the streets don't cross.

I lie on my back, under the linden trees. I sit on the bench, where my mother's friend—the one who was arrested for gunrunning and who died in prison—used to do God's Eyes. I drive by the Hamlet and see it is gone, the whole edifice replaced by a Jamba Juice, which is something my daughter loves anyway. Should I have been informed about all this? Down in Tarzana, the last Orange Julius in southern California finally shuts its doors.

"Tell me again," my daughter says. "Daddy, tell me again about the seasons."

"Go to sleep," I say. We are lying in a hammock stretched across the backyard.

"No, tell me."

She needs a nap, I merely want one. Okay, okay.

"Listen—" the hammock sways—"Spring, summer, winter, fall."

"Hmm," she mumbles around her thumb. "Again."

"Spring, summer, fall, winter."

I almost repeat myself. The hammock sways. As if in the scramblings and half-continuities of experience, there is order after all. The sun pours through the trees and Vivi rotates on her side, curling over her fist. Somewhere across town, my father sticks his belly with needles, injecting himself with Human Growth Hormone. As if he is going to live forever and death were just a superstition to be avoided, the man his own voodoo doll. My mother's body floods with radiation, her tumor shrinks from six centimeters to two. And I am consumed by ghosts, of people I have known and others I have merely guessed at, yet been lucky enough to live with for a while. Shadow spatters like a can of black paint across the patio's far white wall: the last thing I ever look at will probably mean as much to me, though it's impossible it ever could more. The wind picks up and rocks the hammock back and forth. My daughter shivers like a hummingbird. Before she is lost in the provinces of sleep and I beside her, wide awake and also, strictly speaking, dreaming.

Strawberry Is

Strawberry Saroyan

Strawberry is a black and white cat.

Strawberry is eating almonds.

Strawberry is in the honeymoon phase.

Strawberry is a go-go.

Strawberry is fighting her way through the matrix.

Strawberry is throwing her hat over the wall and she's not sure how she's going to get it back.

Strawberry is getting herself together and taking it on the road.

Strawberry is happy to have her name back.

Strawberry is a little bit hungry, and a little bit rock 'n' roll.

Strawberry is exploring the context of no context.

Strawberry is breaking it all down into itty-bitty pieces and making a bikini out of it.

Strawberry is listening to the characters and wondering if they notice.

Strawberry is Tweedledee and Tweedledum.

Strawberry is dancing on the ceiling.

Strawberry thinks Molly Jong-Fast is funny.

Strawberry is wearing Brooks Brothers pajamas.

Strawberry was, and will be.

Strawberry is eating imaginary gumdrops.

Strawberry is up all night.

Strawberry is feeling the fear and doing it anyway.

Strawberry is breaking the fourth wall and trying not to get too bloody in the process.

Strawberry thinks you're wonderful.

Strawberry got home in one piece.

Strawberry is letting go and letting God.

Strawberry is walking the line.

Strawberry is sorting through her phone records to find Bruce Wagner's number.

Strawberry is eating baklava.

Strawberry is counting sheep.

Strawberry is playing blocks.

Strawberry writes on money. And calls it art. And sells it.

Strawberry ate the little green pill.

Strawberry makes time.

Strawberry relented.

Strawberry is howling at the moon.

Strawberry is perfect.

Strawberry is 10 days 2 hours 8 minutes 1 second.

Strawberry is listening to the fat lady sing

Strawberry is hardwired for bliss.

Strawberry is cold as fire, hot as ice.

Strawberry ate the piece of paper with the directions on it.

Strawberry puked it up as pop cult confetti. There were tiny pieces of Farrah Fawcett in it. She gathered them into a pile and put them in a box.

Strawberry is calling the police.

Strawberry wants to be an Alex Katz.

Strawberry is breaking it down so she can put it back together again.

Strawberry scared the black birds who looked like musical notes flying away.

Strawberry is hiding from the paparazzi.

Strawberry is wearing four-inch heels.

Strawberry is on the Hollywood sign, hanging off the "Y."

Strawberry is eating potato chips, barefoot.

Strawberry is interested in what's appropriate. Just kidding.

Strawberry stared into the abyss and found a genuinely usable dining room table.

Strawberry is working out again. You're welcome.

Strawberry really has to get out more.

Strawberry is sounds of bad Britney, Sunset Blvd., midnight, air, dissolving into shards of glitter and eating a cheeseburger.

Strawberry is chocolate-covered pretzels.

Strawberry is enough.

Strawberry is succumbing to the charms of Spanish rice.

Strawberry says yes.

Strawberry is wearing sunglasses at night.

Strawberry is curious.

Strawberry is breathing.

Strawberry is down.

Strawberry is in the back.

Strawberry is: without you I'm nothing.

Strawberry is you.

Strawberry is as Strawberry does.

Strawberry once saw Rodney Bingenheimer alone in a booth at Canter's and looked away.

Strawberry went back to the beginning and started and it was once upon a time with the cats, Chocolate and Powder, remember them?

Strawberry accepts it.

Strawberry shortcake.

Strawberry is trying to put her body back together, but to reach her hand she has to let one knee and an eyeball go.

Strawberry wants to live at The Americana at Brand, and to be very small, and to have a top hat and sequins for her face when she looks in the mirror.

Strawberry is talking to air.

Strawberry is elementary.

Strawberry looked and saw and believed it.

Strawberry is an American Express card.

Strawberry's psyche is made of chocolate.

Strawberry is in the midst of it.

Strawberry is looking over there and going: hi.

Strawberry feels like Ali McGraw.

Strawberry wants to make it clear.

Strawberry told you already and doesn't understand why you don't understand.

Strawberry is afraid she'll be blocked. And then what will she do? Will she be in a corner?

Strawberry cried today.

Strawberry admitted it.

Strawberry is in the silence of a room. A car went by.

Strawberry likes the pink and the yellow in the painting.

Strawberry is a splash of purple.

Strawberry remembers looking for the Cracker Jack prize.

Strawberry believes that she must and will do it, even though it's impossible.

Strawberry is deep down in the hole. There's only a little bit of light.

Strawberry isn't going to go too far. Don't worry.

Strawberry wore the Marni shirt even though it was dirty.

Strawberry worried about money until she cut off her leg.

Strawberry thinks towels are interesting

Strawberry let herself go. No one noticed.

Strawberry's voice cracked.

Strawberry ran into the room but everyone was gone.

Strawberry is cranking it up and singing along.

Strawberry is driving.

Strawberry is sitting down, immobile, don't stop, now do, oh forget it.

Strawberry went to the moon and back and wrote a note to the cleaning lady.

Strawberry doesn't care anymore.

Strawberry saw the cup and the page and her jeans and candy.

Strawberry flew like the cuckoo and it was beautiful so high up in the tree, on the telephone pole, remembering eucalyptus like it was yesterday.

Strawberry stapled it together.

Strawberry is patterns and light and your mother.

Strawberry is wrong.

Strawberry is right.

Strawberry is keys and paper and sandals and an old-fashioned address book.

Strawberry is 2 across and 1 down.

Strawberry is fading and then coming back into sight.

Strawberry doesn't speak English.

Strawberry is 15–love.

Strawberry is 30–15.

Strawberry saw stars.

Learn to Drive Trucks   Big Money

Henry Alcalay

THEY RUSHED ME TO LENOX HILL HOSPITAL AND YANKED OUT MY appendix. Then they said I had to have a roommate. Late that night he died. I should have been asleep but I was up, I'd been given Demerol, the worst drug of all; I've played around with opiates enough to know the good stuff from the fake. The moaning began around midnight, louder and louder it grew, almost musical. I pressed the button, no one came. The moaning was replaced by a rasping gasp. Help is on the way, I said, but we were on our own. Where they'd cut my flank felt like it was on fire. The rasping gave way to a high-pitched sighing, like this aria I'd heard on the radio, which turned out to be an ad for Ragu meat sauce. Then he fell silent and I wondered if he'd died. Two orderlies stomped in and turned on the light, arguing about their card game. You'll lick the dingleberries from my butt before I believe you had a full house, one said to the other. I called out for morphine. White boy must be talking in his sleep, they laughed, and slapped palms and removed my roommate in his bathrobe.

I stayed home a month and had my food delivered. Percocet around the clock. Time stopped and I felt like a sailor on a sub—nothing I can do from here, might as well relax.

I first met Mary in a candy store while buying *The Daily News*. Later, when my friends would ask about her, they would kid me it was appropriate we had met in such a place since she was 'a piece of candy' or 'a sweet-looking thing' or whatever they might say to reduce her to a plaything and console themselves it hadn't happened to them. I paid little attention to their cracks and when I looked in their eyes saw only envy.

They knew better than me it was just luck we met. Every morning I'd to go to the store around the corner for the papers. Some days I had exact change. I'd get up at eight and brush my teeth and dunk my head and walk in with it dripping. Once, I couldn't sleep and went in at five. The morning sky was still blue-black, all the lights were on and the smell of fresh-brewed coffee hit me when I opened the door. Half a dozen old men were already there, drinking coffee and smoking and gabbing over which horses to bet on at OTB that day. *The Times* delivery truck pulled up and the driver let the clutch out with a bang. The guy in back heaved off the wire-bound bundles and came inside to give the newsie his receipt. Taking a Milky Way for free, he climbed back on the truck. Though I made ten times as much and worked in a plush office, not until I was thirty would I stop wanting his job.

The morning I met Mary I went in at eight. The radio said a hurricane was coming. The newspapers agreed. Not having change I gave the clerk a five. Beside me stood a woman I thought I'd seen before; rough strawberry hair hung down to her coccyx, cut square across the bottom like a shower curtain. Her shoulder blades hoisted up her T-shirt, her ass was as small as a child's. You can be arrested if you smack a stranger's butt. I leaned over the counter like something on the other side concerned me so I could see her face and her eyes caught mine; deep set, large and indigo, they appeared lit from within. It struck me you could go your whole life without seeing eyes like that. Worse, you could see them once and never see them again.

The clerk, for some reason, thought she was with me and took the price of her Parliaments out of the money I'd put down.

Hey, what happened? I asked him, in a voice I tried to make soft and hoarse like I'd been up all night, singing or making love.

He looked at me, then at her. Jeez, I'm sorry, he said, squinting from the smoke of the cigar jammed between his teeth, I taut you was together. He saw the change she'd put down and handed me some singles. You two'd make a good couple, you know it? he said, his eyes moving between us. He signaled me to step back to stop dripping on his counter.

Sorry, she turned to me, Guess he didn't see it.

That's okay, I told her, Not like it was your fault. I tried to meet her eyes but my gaze dropped to her chin. A thin blue vein was visible just beneath her skin, which, the way it reinforced the fact she was just flesh and blood, scared me even more. I squeezed past her for the door, remembering what Errol Flynn said: the woman always chooses, it just looks the other way.

I stood outside, leaning on a parking meter, the cool metal soothing, wishing I were her dog tied there, no explaining needed. Low-hanging clouds went scudding past and the light had a jaundiced cast. The wind blew and debris shot past, the streetlights along Second Avenue creaked, swinging with each gust. The sense of impending catastrophe made me feel connected to everyone who went by.

Trying to decide if I should go to work, I lied when she appeared. I still couldn't look her in the eyes.

God, don't do that, she waved her hand, Take the day off, make it a long weekend, what have you got to lose? She'd stopped and was looking at me. Okay, good, I thought.

Cigarette? I offered, extending my Camels, hoping she'd come closer. In my other hand I had matches.

No thanks, she said, holding up her fresh pack. You go ahead, though. I had this little skit I'd thought up, how to light up in a typhoon. Plugging a Camel between my lips, I pulled the matchbook apart so the matches dangled. LEARN TO DRIVE TRUCKS BIG MONEY BE YOUR OWN BOSS it said. There was a number to call.

I wondered if I should I keep them. I lit two matches and with them lit the whole book. With a whoosh and some sparks it flared into a flame, which I held to my cigarette.

Hurricanes don't scare me, I said, tossing the matchbook away when it began burning my hand. Nine years ago today Hendrix died, I said. You're a good listener, I added, amazed she had hung around this long.

What's your name? she asked. Boy, when they ask that, you're in.

Walter. What's yours?

Mary, she said, extending her hand, cool and dry, no jewelry, her grip such as you'd use on a steering wheel.

The wind cries Mary, I explained. Her smile became a grimace.

Where are you from? I asked.

Albany.

What was there to say to that? Albany, no kidding, I said as if I'd just heard everyone there had been killed. How about a nice hot chocolate? I said. That place over there on the corner—indicating with my chin—has the best hot chocolate in Manhattan.

The pork store?

Well, one *in* from the corner. Moby's Luncheonette there. How about it?

No, I don't want hot chocolate, sounding like a little girl. I was confused where that left me.

Don't want it now or don't want it ever?

She laughed, which for some reason made me think again of Jimi Hendrix. He knew how to talk to girls, you'd think, just from how he sang, his voice husky and mocking, chuckling between phrases, but when I saw him on Dick Cavett, he could hardly speak at all. He leaned forward in his chair and spoke in mumbling bursts and you knew if he talked to you like that and he wasn't famous, you would walk away.

I can't today, Mary said, How about another time?

She paused, watching my reaction. A gust of wind lifted her long heavy hair and held it out like a flag. I'm not just giving you the brush, she said.

We exchanged phone numbers, writing our secret digits down on scraps torn from my newspaper.

I live over there, Mary said, pointing north and across Second Avenue. Right over that store, second floor.

Mortuary supplies?

No, next door, Trusses and Supports.

I live over there, I said, vaguely pointing west along Eighty-third Street. The way the wind was picking up I had this urge to shout.

I was going to leave and then it hit me, from the way she stood. Hey! I said, You're the mask girl, I just realized. She laughed. Ha, I said, I thought so.

The mask girl had been on a ton of magazine covers that summer, always in the same pose and always the same clothes, just a toga, really, leaning forward with her legs spread like she was challenging the viewer. Covering her eyes was a slick black mask but you could see her mouth and cheekbones and tell she was a knockout. She was everywhere for a couple of months, like a midday cloud that drifts across the sun, and then she was gone.

I ran up four flights to my apartment and to the bathroom mirror to see what she saw. My hair was dry and wind tossed but the corners of my eyes had crusts, which dunking hadn't washed off. Fuck, I thought, before I saw it didn't matter. Sitting at my desk I copied Mary's number from the back page of *The News* into my address book. Looking at the numbers I could tell how my hands trembled as I wrote while she dictated. I tore that page from the paper, folded it carefully and put it in my drawer. I wanted to always have it, and when it was old and yellow I could take it out and be reminded of that day I'd gone around myself and done something I was afraid to.

For a while I just read the paper. They were still squeezing the last drops of juice from the weeks-old story of Thurman Munson's fiery death. Baseball would never be the same, if you believed how they told it. In front of my building my ancient landlady swept the sidewalk with a withered broom. What are you doing? I felt like calling down, Once the hurricane arrives it will sweep everything clean. Later, after it had gotten dark, the rain falling in sheets and the wind complaining, I realized I had borrowed from the storm whatever boldness I had marshaled in speaking to Mary. But I had no idea what would happen next and found myself wishing it would last for days.

A week later I called Mary and asked if she'd like to have dinner at the Isle of Capri, down the street from Bloomingdales.

The Isle of Capri? she said.

I just like the name. They have little palm trees.

Okay, she agreed.

The night of our date she looked different from when we had met; women always do. The second time you see them is like meeting someone new. She had on makeup and heels and a blue silk dress. She put up her hand and a Checker cab stopped.

The waiter brought us menus. Have the veal, I said, best veal in the city, which it surely wasn't but I enjoyed that line. It's from *The Godfather*, that scene in the restaurant where Michael Corleone kills the crooked cop. I liked using lines other men have used while being strong. After that I let her do the talking, my only technique; it's hard not being boring explaining yourself. I like keeping quiet, leaving room for them to overestimate me if they want.

She talked about modeling. First you have to know your colors, she said. What are yours? I asked. Doesn't matter, she explained. She said she was back in New York only a few months after two years in Paris: you signed with an agency and they sent you there. When you had enough tear sheets they brought you to New York and expected you to work. Every year they culled the crop and tossed the deadwood. Well, everyone does that, I said, we're doing it right here. She said she had a boyfriend in Paris and that we should just be friends.

I sensed that was coming or she might not have been so friendly when we met: much less much riding on it. Anyway, the last thing I rely on is the words to fill me in. That was fine with me. The pills I was on had killed my libido—opiates do that but they give you something else: the ability to absorb affection in any form it's given, as if once your sex drive's gone, your ego's gone too. I've fallen in love more times in that state than I ever have while sober.

I got home and lay across my bed and lit a Camel. That first puff as it goes down, how can you even think of anything else? I wondered if we really would be friends and would I meet her girlfriends and were they models too? Glancing at the floor I saw I'd left the paper open to a picture of Robert Garwood. Now, *he* was news, if you asked me; captured by the Vietcong in 1965, now in the fall of '79, six years after the other POWs, he'd just been released. The other POWs were calling him a traitor, saying that during their imprisonment he had informed on them and wanted to stay behind. Leaning off my bed, I looked at his picture, wondering if he liked the attention, if he was glad to be back, but the newsprint was grainy and it was hard to tell. He told one reporter the only song the North Vietnamese guards let the prisoners sing was "Que Sera, Sera."

I crushed my cigarette on the floor and lit another and went into this reverie where I saw myself leaving Xenon surrounded by Mary and a bunch of other models and one or two guys, all of us on our way for eggs and champagne after having danced the night away. And Garwood is with us too, his fame such potent currency he's welcome everywhere, strangers only too happy to cavort in its glow. Bobby! One of the girls with us cries, Bobby! Come on! Let's go! He jogs up to join us, clumping along in his canvas lace-ups, jungle fatigues, and hat. With his new pot belly and sandy thinning hair he looks like the kind of guy who could tell you just what's what at the feed and farm store. Of course his teeth are awful, made worse next to ours. As we hit the sidewalk a photographer from *The Post* raises his camera. Bobby drapes his arms around those closest to him as the flash goes off; see, he seems to be saying, plenty of fame to go around. In one arm he carries a teak walking stick he carved during his years in the jungle. Around his other forearm an asp circles and hisses.

At the canopy of the Brasserie, a small band has gathered to welcome us; half a dozen busboys and dishwashers bang on cans and colanders, trying to figure out the words to "Que Sera, Sera." Passing taxis chip in with their muted horns. But who really knows the words and at times the serenade lapses into something sounding like the second half of "Hey, Jude;" *na na na nananana nananana*. Walter, Mary tugs on my arm until I'm facing a pale-skinned brunette with eyes the color of raw honey that glow like a Weimaraner's. Walter this is . . . \ Le Le Hiep; she doesn't speak any English and needs someone to show her around New York for a few days. Garwood, rather than a chair, squats by the side of our table, shoveling food into his face with his right hand. Bobby, I say, and he looks up and I want him to know that though I hang around with models and think champagne goes with eggs, I'm still a serious person and I ask him, What feels better, Bobby, all the fame in the world or a quiet room with a clean pipe full of opium? Dung hand, he explains, holding up his left. Left hand to wipe with, right hand to eat, looking at me unimpressed.

The next day Mary called to thank me for dinner and to suggest that the following Friday she come by and take me to this place she'd heard about where boys boxed in a ring while people dined. They sweat in your food, they bleed in your beer, she described it.

Tablecloths? I asked.

I should think, she said.

The night she was due to arrive I wondered what to wear. Maybe a suit but I wore suits all week. Each day in *The News* Garwood wore a suit. But something was off, I noticed, studying his picture; the lapels are tiny, the ties two inches wide. Then it dawned on me he was wearing the clothes he owned before he was captured, clothes from 1965. He was captured just eleven days before he was due to rotate home. An orderly, he'd been driving a jeep and had just dropped off some general and was on his way back to base when three Vietcong surrounded his vehicle. One of them was a woman. Maybe that's why he stopped. Now with this business that maybe he's a traitor the government won't shell out for new clothes. They wouldn't even fly him home; the Vietnamese sent him as far as Bangkok and from there KLM flew him to New York for free.

Mary arrived bearing paperwhites, dressed in a faded pink jumpsuit under a bright yellow slicker. I liked that we were the same height—rangy girls my size make me want to wrestle. Not so much that night, though. I was glad to see her. Man, I love the way these things look but they sure make you sweat, I said, helping her off with her slicker. Hanging it, I sniffed it but nothing. I poured us some red wine and we sat on my sofa.

Nice place, she said, gazing around. It was just a studio apartment on the fourth floor of a five-floor walkup, filled with ottomans, credenzas, settees and two couches, an elaborate stereo, a Fender bass guitar, and a Fender amp. It looked more like a showroom than a place to live. I'd had the bass for three years and had never learned to play; sometimes I'd put on the Police or the Stones and lazily thump along—with the volume high enough I could pretend I belonged.

Oh, you play the bass, Mary said.

No, that belongs to a friend.

Where do you sleep? Does one of these sofas turn into a bed?

Actually, I sleep in the other room, I said, grateful for the chance to surprise her.

What other room?

I was living here when the studio next door became available.

We had to step out into the hall to get to it. Here I had a queen-sized bed, a night table, a love seat, and an unpainted wood dresser, which I'd bought at one of those unpainted furniture stores New York was once dotted with. This one was on Second Avenue, just around the corner. One day I watched it burn. The heat was intense, I felt it on my face, watching from my rooftop two hundred feet away. Looming over the bed was a potted corn plant. Seven feet tall, it looked like a palm tree. Hanging everywhere, in the apartment's one tiny closet as well as on all the walls, were perhaps three dozen suits. Mary moved along inspecting them like paintings. So many suits, she exclaimed, pinching the fabric. She glanced at what was on the night table: *Moby Dick,* some *Archie* comics, *Love Letters to Pat* by Richard Nixon, a book on stain removal. Finished, she plopped down on the sofa.

What is it you do again, your family has a business?

Something like that.

She opened her hand and gestured that I should continue. I rubbed two fingers together in that way that means money. That kind of business, I said.

Doing what? she insisted.

Some of us sell insurance and others set fires.

Mary laughed like she was supposed to: the idea that I could carry on like that.

I took another sip of wine. I'd taken some pills but not enough to make the leap to where nothing matters. I figured I'd get more when they ran out. I'm in a funny place, I said, like I've stopped moving forward.

Because of your operation?

More like I just don't care.

Everyone feels like that sometimes.

No, but I seem to like it. Like giving up implies a sort of wisdom.

Like you're above it all?

I nodded.

You're too young to feel that way, she said. Not good.

By the time George Harrison was my age the Beatles had already broken up.

And then he kept going.

That's true, I agreed, and looked in her eyes. Her pupils were enormous, a good sign, I knew; big like that they're letting you in, they can't get enough. Look in someone's eyes and all you see is color, they're not sure at all.

You're giving up on yourself, my closest friend had scolded me years before when I called him up to say I was going to work for my father. *You're kissing your dreams goodbye.* I got off the phone convinced I'd never speak to him again. Things didn't turn out that way either.

Let's go back in the other room, I said to Mary, I have something to show you. The thought came to me that thinking is useless, only action counts. How can you know how you feel until your mind stops working?

I'll bring this, she said, clutching her wineglass. A fire truck blared past on Second Avenue, followed, moments later, by another.

We work 'round the clock, I joked.

Mary resumed her seat on the sofa. Odd stains I couldn't account for dotted the back. The thought of having it cleaned seemed such a drag: find someone to call, have them come and get it. The idea alone was tiring. I took a wooden cigar box from my desk and sat beside her. Let's look at these pictures, I said, and opened the lid. The rich sweet smell of the cigars it once held wafted up to tweak us. I'd filled it with photos of me from when I was an infant up to age twenty or so. There were some from when I was two, bundled in a snowsuit, romping in the snow in front of the big old stone and timber house where I grew up. Far off in the background looms a large black dog. Against a nearby tree a sled leans on its side. There were pictures from when I was five, sitting beside my sister on a concrete seawall in Miami Beach, both of us in bright yellow jumpsuits, competing, perhaps, with the sun, competing, perhaps, with each other. There were pictures in which I was ten at summer camp, where I squint into the sun, the middle of my face a mass of freckles. In my teenage pictures, the freckles have disappeared.

I hadn't planned on showing her those pictures. To judge by her reaction, it was a good idea—it increased our rapport without the need to speak. We were nearly through when I started wishing that at the bottom, as if hidden, were pictures of me in fatigues with a rifle in my hands. Behind me would be helicopters and some tents and palm trees. She'd ask what they were and I would hesitate, picking one and staring at it as if words failed me.

Besides Robert Garwood, this was the year of the first big Vietnam movies; *Apocalypse Now* and *The Deer Hunter* and the first best-sellers, *Going After Cacciato, A Rumor of War* and like with all epics, romance and fantasy had been grafted onto what was must have been a terrifying and sordid experience. But now the war was all romantic: trees the size of buildings, Jim Morrison crooning as jets dispatch napalm, opium and acid, incense and helicopters, waterskiing, surfing, a friendly little game of Russian Roulette . . .

The summer before I'd seen this guy, my age more or less, sitting shirtless on a couch in a sweltering tenement on the Lower East Side, both of us waiting for the dealer to return. He had the sort of stillness that has nothing about it of a conscious choice. I stared at his scar, a thick raised pink ribbon encircling his torso like the shadow of a noose, as if his whole chest had been lifted out and put back, as you might excise a piece of wedding cake. What happened? I asked. Vietnam, he said, no more intonation than if he'd said *vanilla*. Later, waiting for the bus downstairs on First Avenue, I wondered if I'd ever run into him again.

I imagined telling Mary I'd been there, asking her if she'd like to meet my buddies. Mary, this is . . . Dugan. He and I went through hell together, the hell of Vietnam. He's visiting New York for a few days and needs someone to show him around.

The boxing took place in what was once a sanitation department garage. Salt stains marked the walls, though the piles were gone. They'd left the lockers in one corner where the fighters changed. We could hear the slam of their metal doors. Donovan, our waiter, said it was rude to watch; sit down, please, he urged and offered deviled eggs. They were really boys, like Mary had said; lithe teenagers with fair skin, lean, with hairless torsos, Latins, most of them. The tables, round and intimate, were lit by candles. The garage was built out on the river on the West side, broken pilings just beside it marching into darkness.

Who're you rooting for? I asked when the introductions started.

She put down her soup spoon and studied the contestants. That one, he's cuter, she said, and I felt a pang of envy for the one she wished to see hurt.

The first fight began and the squeaking of their shoes on the resined canvas mingled with the exclamations of the crowd. We heard the blows rather than saw them, that's how fast it happens; a thud, a thwack, a stinging swish and one would recoil, a dazed look in his eyes. Then he would move forward: what choice did he have? Each fight was short, four or six rounds, though how could it have seemed so to those being pummeled. Six fights altogether, and after every one a man with a mop climbed in the ring to clean up spit and blood. I would take that job, I thought. We ate lobster bisque and steak and drank bottles of wine. Ravenous, we held up our plates and yelled at Donovan for more.

Afterward we couldn't find a cab. I felt like complaining but made myself shut up. It was raining as it had each night since we had met; New York was attaining a tropical aspect. We walked south beneath the overpass that runs along the river where the ocean liners dock and we stayed dry. Wharf rats, I said, but we saw none. The ropes of the big boats had those tins to keep them off. Hard to believe they worked. A ship was getting ready to depart. Streamers were flying, people milling, getting on and off. When the boat's steam whistle went we felt it in our chests. Odd that it's leaving now, I said and Mary nodded. Let's go see, I said, and we went up the crowded gangplank. The ship's officer on top gaped at Mary, leaning into her like he might make a pass. I took in his uniform and wondered how he felt, if it added or detracted, then peered at his clipboard and picked a name as if we'd come to see them off. I told it to him and he let us pass. He would have anyway, I thought, and turned to see his eyes still watching Mary.

Let's find the bar, Mary said. We went below deck. Every other room hosted a party. Someday we should do this, she said, sail around the world.

We could leave tonight, stow away, I said, buy new clothes on board. I want one of those hats like the Captain from the Captain and Tenille.

When we arrive in England you could torch the ship, she said.

Or halfway across.

People were looking at us: the women watching Mary to see what she had, the men looking at her and then at me to see where my luck came from. A man in his thirties in a tux with sandy hair falling boyishly, charmlessly, over his eyes came tumbling out of a cabin, champagne glass in hand. Hello, he burped, nearly bumping into Mary. He looked at her and crumpled slightly, as if he'd lost his balance. Then he looked at me. Whoa, he said, stepping sideways. Where's the photographers?

We kept moving till we found a bar. Visitors? the bartender asked, placing two napkins. You have fifteen minutes. We ordered whiskey sours. That was pretty sexy, don't you think? I said, when the glow from the whiskey had kicked in.

She narrowed her eyes. The boxers?

Two half-naked men trying to kill each other, hot bright lights, everyone watching. There you are, on your own, with whatever you're made of. I took a sip and looked at her.

Do go on, she said.

I liked looking at the women, some of them, the way they were screaming, especially when a fighter was in trouble. So aroused, their eyes sparkled like lakes on fire. You can learn more about human nature from a prizefight than from all the books ever written.

Mary put her hand on mine, resting on the bar. God, your hands are soft, she said, especially for a man. Her pupils were tiny, even when she smiled.

Mary's boyfriend, Feppler, came from France to visit. I liked him right away. He had that pale pallor Genet speaks of in convicts who never see the sun and low-voltage energy as if instead of a heart he had a filament. He was probably thirty and wore timeless clothes, chinos and zippered jackets and button-down white shirts. Mary put him at ease by telling him, Walter's afraid of girl germs. He remained a month and made extra money filling in at police lineups. The demand is there, he said, anyone can do it. But you have money, I presume? he asked me one day over vermouth. I enjoy what Balzac said: you can run through your money but you can't run through what you're made of. His smile was coy and slightly artificial but he only spoke when he had something to say.

The demand is there; New York in the late seventies was a city without order, as if an invading army had ousted the authorities and then moved on as well. Cops stayed in their cars their whole shift. Mayor Koch was useless: How'm I doin', how'm I'm doin'? squawking like a Perdue Oven Stuffer with a clothespin on his nose. Each time you went out you had but a fair chance of coming home unscathed. In a listless effort to tamp down the madness, as if junkies were the problem, methadone was made available free to anyone who wanted it. You could have a habit or just say you did; they took blood and if they found anything at all you were in. Clinics sprang up everywhere, money to be made.

Opiates get a bad rap. They don't addict very easily—you have to work at it for months—nor are they hard to kick: a ten day bout of flu, a month of the blues, and then you're your old self again. Nor, other than constipation, do they cause health issues. Which is why staying off's so hard: once you've been through it you know how little there is to fear.

The exception is methadone. Rather than a rush it makes you feel whole: nothing more to want, nothing left to prove. Compared to junk and morphine it lasts three times as long. The Nazis synthesized it in 1944 when they ran out of opium. Very hard to kick though, compared to other opiates: a month of the flu and malaise for four months.

The clinic I signed on at was in Harlem, Madison and 105th. Not a particularly rough neighborhood other than the projects across the street. I got there at eight every morning and then went back home to shower for work. One day in November I arrived to find a hold on my dose.

Dr. Bhjakura wants to see you, the nurse in the closet where the methadone was dispensed said, setting up her orange juice behind the dutch door. Mascara from her eyelashes had drifted onto one cheek.

First give me my dose.

I can't give you anything without his permission. Go sit in the lounge and I'll call you, motioning to the person behind me to step up to the window.

Dr. Bhjakura made me wait an hour. This is the life we've chosen, I thought, remembering what Lee Strassberg as Meyer Lansky tells Michael in *The Godfather* when Michael starts complaining that his boys are getting whacked. I read *The Daily News.* Garwood was out of the picture; he'd been gone for weeks, replaced by news of the hostages the Ayatollah seized in Iran. I wondered if already they were falling in love with their captors. In someone's office a radio played: *if you like pina coladas and getting caught in the rain . . .*

Summoned to the doctor's office, I headed down the hall. He nearly stood when I entered before remembering himself. Sit, he indicated, using that hand gesture trainers do with dogs. I couldn't keep from gaping at his tie, flabbergasted by its size. At its thickest part, it looked eight inches wide. The red material from which it was made—emblazoned with dollar signs and Hebrew-looking letters which said over and over, Mazel Tov—was so bulky it appeared nearly quilted. When he stood to put his coffee mug on the shelf behind him it dangled past his knees. Just the knot alone would have astonished me; it was the size of those seat cushions on motorboats which double as flotation devices. I nearly burst out laughing but it was also sad. Someone had given him the tie as a joke but the doctor, not understanding, was wearing it in earnest, imagining it looked good.

The urine sample . . . you left last week . . . came back . . . with morphine traces, he said, his perfect, high-pitched English coming in lilting bursts.

I guess this was bound to happen, I said, remembering that those were the dying words of Dicky Chapelle, a *National Geographic* photographer who'd had her throat slashed by exploding shrapnel while covering the war in Vietnam. Along with the account was a picture of a priest giving her last rites: her eyes are open, she's aware of her life spilling into the dirt. How strange, I'd thought, to be lying down while everyone else is up. And where did the priest come from? I supposed they'd choppered him in as they did beer and steaks and letters from home.

I glanced at the doctor, at most eight or nine years older than me, in his middle thirties. Sometimes in the waiting room grumbling recipients liked to say the doctors, being foreign, were inferior, but I disagreed—all of them had come a long way to get here and they wouldn't stay long. A year or two and they'd move on, this place but an odd gray shadow if they remembered it at all. They'd come from far away—Mexico, Sri Lanka, Pakistan, the Phillipines—and must have been stunned to see so many young Americans throwing away with both hands everything they had come so far to attain.

Poppy seeds, I said to the doctor.

Poppy . . . seeds? Excuse me?

From bagels. Poppy seeds on the bagels I eat for breakfast Sunday mornings. Sort of an American tradition. That's why my urine shows morphine traces.

Dr. Bhjakura and I stared at one another, then I dropped my gaze. In another office, someone laughed and coughed, and laughed and coughed again. I looked around his office. Rather than diplomas and framed certificates, he had pictures of himself playing polo, galloping on horses or holding trophies with his teammates. Everyone was smiling, not needing to be told. From East 105th Street, eleven floors below, came the sudden sound of a jack hammer. It erupted briefly, stopped, then went on in earnest for a while. In some way its strident, ringing jangle evoked in me a surge of good cheer, why, I had no idea.

It made me want to leap out of my chair, clap Dr. Bhjakura on the back and tell him not to fear, that things would work out so well for each of us that someday these mornings would seem the keepsake of strangers. The passing sounds of a car radio, a smell catching us unawares, a color glimpsed unexpectedly before fading from view, and briefly, but only briefly, these days would reappear. Beyond this, I wished to assure him, nothing will remain.

Tell the nurse . . . I said to give you your dose . . . give her another urine sample . . . and we will speak next week. Turning his chair around, adjusting his elephantine tie, he poured some tea from a thermos, then opened his *New York Times*.

Downstairs it was cold out. The morning was shot. I followed a knot of fellow recipients around the corner and into a run down general store-bodega on Madison. LEGS SHAVED, $8, said the hand-painted sign outside the beauty parlor. We crowded in together, some of the women pushing strollers. Once inside we spread out. I studied red cans of condensed milk for a while, then moved to a revolving metal rack stuffed with old records still in plastic; Vic Damone, Roger Miller, Patti Page, Jan and Dean. I bought *The Ventures' Greatest Hits*, and pulling up the collar of my pea coat and putting on dark glasses, started walking home.

I was on my block when I spotted Mary. She was with her pal Cynthia, whom I'd already met. Cynthia was swarthy, vaguely Persian though not really. She was from Santa Barbara and, she said, old money. Her dark satin hair had an air of tensile strength. The Witch That Won't Burn, Feppler took to calling her. They were walking towards me but hadn't seen me yet. Shoving my hands in my pocket I bent my head and moved to the middle of the sidewalk so they would have to make room. Growing closer I began moaning loudly. I was almost to them when I yanked off my sunglasses.

Oh, my god, it's you, Mary said and started laughing. We thought you were some nut and were going to cross the street. Very funny, wiseguy, she said, and punched my arm. What are you doing anyway; wanna come eat with us?

I have to get to my office.

Hey, that's right; how come you're not at work?

How do you know I'm not? I said, and she faltered a bit and in that instant I had an urge to tell her everything: my fear of girl germs and where I went each morning, and Dr. Bhjakura's endearing air of empathy and disdain. But it quickly passed—things were fine the way they were. Want one? I asked, extending my pack of cigarettes. Silently Cynthia shook her head; she spoke less than Calvin Coolidge. Mary took one and I lit it for her.

Jesus, look at you, she said. What's she so happy about, I wondered. Her pupils were vast like a dog getting a biscuit. Sticking her cigarette in her mouth, she bounced up and down and threw punches at me. We're going to take boxing lessons, she said, sounding strangulated from talking with her lips clamped. Cynthia met Sugar Ray Leonard's trainer at 54 the other night and he said he'd give us private sessions. He says in four weeks he'll put us in the best shape of our lives. You should come with us, she finished, still bobbing, already winded.

I'm sure that's what he wants, I said.

Well, I mean, that way if he tries anything you can protect us, Mary snickered.

I had to admit it sounded sexy: wearing boxing trunks, my torso exposed, taking harder punches than he'd dare throw at the girls; had I a libido I'd have said yes in an instant. Years later in a karate class, sparring with a woman for the first time, I was not surprised to find I was erect beneath my gi.

I should probably shove off for my office, I told Mary. I watched them walk off, shoulder bumping close, finishing my cigarette on the deserted street while the wind blew through the bare sycamores where in all my New York years I'd never seen a bird build a nest to lay her eggs.

The virtual calendar subtracts.

Examining my maps: no sex

till Nova Scotia I predict.

(Becker, page 15)

Picture Postcard

John Fandel

1.

An aged greenthumb townee
keeps a patch of earth
this side of the bridge into town
flowering all summer long.
Such lilies! Spirea! Dahlias!
And golly the hollyhocks!

2.

This morning's blue gentian stopped me
& butterflies, three whites' worth
of awe, no-flutter their own
awe for blue spires, mute song.
The holy happens, their "hail-ya's!"
Hallelujahs of hollyhocks.

3.

A stream of Lucernes, Avalons,
Civics, Infinitis,
on this trafficked bridge to town;
for blue-and-whites, be a walker,
silent, not a talker;
stop to hear, on your own,
white peals in blue spires, affinities
with, under-stream, silent, three swans.

Spanish Lesson

I nearly stepped on *noun*
on an old rose 3 x 5 card.,,
picked it up, turned it over:
un sustantivo;

10 paces, another index:
adjective / un adjectivo:

pace out, 10, a third:
mood, flip:
un estado de emoción.

My "Spanish lesson" over,
pacing on, I recalled
reading that Tennyson's friends
jotted on slips of paper,
pink, things to versify
and dropped them on the path
to his hidden versing-hut,
to inspire "Alfred's genius."

"Pen a slight one-liner,
Mood piece, adjective noun,
charged with *emoción* . . ."

OPEN CITY

I: Laureate Lord Idyllic . . .

Click

Arrived at the Doctor's office.
While waiting, I tried my hand:

*M*otivation *O*m: *O* roseate *D*oom.

Snowing and Knowing

Refrigerator White
looks out and sees snow "White

as 'I am,' colder tho—
last heard, 10 below."

Two whites, not the same.
The shading, Who can name?

How is one to know?
Can you tell day to night?
Fire from flame?

Mused

Long concealed
congealed.

Lo, diamonds! So coal.
Et alii. Soul.

Something more, as well?
:
asphalt, asphodel.

Piecemeal

Caedra Scott-Flaherty

I REARRANGE THE LIVING ROOM FURNITURE BEFORE MY HUSBAND wakes up. Move the couch up against the front wall so that he'll be able to see the TV better. So that he'll be distracted by this and won't notice the absence of the fingers on my left hand.

Three fingers fell into the sink while I was washing my face last night. I hid them under my pillow and slept restlessly. Before rearranging the furniture this morning, I placed the fingers on the top shelf of the utility closet in the kitchen. Right next to the laundry detergent.

My Fingers

I used them for balance. Up against my lover's shower wall. Down on his mattress. Holding the cigarette out the window on the drive back to my husband.

They were more curious than other parts of me. Curious and naive and slender.

"I like watching you write," my lover said. He came up behind me and I set the pen down. "No, keep writing. You hold the pen wrong. I like it."

I picked it up.

"Just keep writing." He bent down over me, running his hands up my thighs, lifting my skirt as his fingers slid between my legs. "I love when you do things wrong," he whispered. "You know that."

I make my husband breakfast. Scrambled eggs with American cheese. Two pieces of wheat toast, unbuttered. A cup of coffee. He walks into the kitchen as I'm dishing the eggs onto a plate.

"Looks like a whole new room out there." I hear his chair scrape the linoleum. Hear him sit down.

The bread pops out of the toaster. I reach for it and my left hand falls onto the counter. I quickly tuck it into my apron pocket and then place the toast on his plate. I bring him his breakfast, hiding my left arm behind my back as I set the plate in front of him.

"It looks great."

As he eats, I go to the utility closet. Hidden by its open door, I lift the left hand out of my pocket and place it on the top shelf, between the fingers and the laundry detergent. I grab a sponge, close the door and smile at my husband.

He smiles back at me, bits of scrambled eggs poking out of the corners of his mouth. "This is delicious. Thank you."

I put the new sponge next to the sink. I turn around, crossing my arms behind me, and watch him eat.

My Hands

I used them to summon him. Up out of sleep. Down onto me. Away from the bedroom window when I heard my husband pulling into the driveway early.

They were always cold and dry.

"I don't think it's a circulation problem," my lover said.

We were leaning against the side of my house. He took my hands and pulled them up under his sweater. Pressed my palms against his skin, always too warm. Holding me by the wrists, we moved up his chest, around to his back and then down his front. We slipped into his pants. "Here." His belt dug into my knuckles as he bent into my hair. "I think you just want to be kept warm."

When my husband finishes eating his breakfast, he carries his empty plate over to me and sets it by the sink. He kisses my forehead and then my cheek. "Have a great day, okay?"

I adjust my arms behind my back.

"See you later." He walks to the door. He is almost out before he turns around and leans against the frame. "You look beautiful this morning." He smiles at my face. "I love you."

I smile back.

He nods and closes the door behind him. I hear his shoes against the pavement. Hear the engine starting up before the car door slams shut.

I wash the dishes. I lean on my left elbow and scrub with my right hand. It is uncomfortable. As I bend to put the plate in the drying rack, my left arm falls off at the shoulder. It drops onto the kitchen floor. Bending to pick it up, I notice an accumulation of crumbs under the sink. I carry the arm over to the utility closet and set it on the middle shelf, behind the folded dishrags I take out the broom and dustpan. The floors need a good sweeping.

My Arms

I used them like guns. Up against his temples. Down into his chest. When I wanted something and knew exactly how to get it, fast.

They were aggressive and calculating. They knew how to wrap things up, how to twist things at just the right angle.

"Hold my neck." My lover had me up against the garage wall. Between the hanging saw and the hammers. His arms hooked under my thighs, held me up and moved me. I was bobbing and weightless, gulping cement and gasoline and rubber. He bit me at the shoulder. Left my skin wet. "Shhhhhh."

When I finish sweeping the crumbs into one pile, I move into the dining room. I sweep around the long table clockwise, leaving small piles of dust at every corner.

I drop the dustpan in front of each of the piles. Hold it steady with my left foot and sweep it up with my right hand. It takes longer than usual, but when I'm done, the floors look especially fresh and wide. Except in the living room.

I put the broom and dustpan back in the utility closet and pull out the vacuum. Drag it along the linoleum, across the wood, and plug it into the living room wall. The rug is shallow and soft and every stroke leaves a mark. I create circles, swirls, and zigzags. I erase them. I vacuum for too long and when I'm done the room smells like burning plastic.

I drag the vacuum back across the wood, along the linoleum. As I put it against the utility closet wall, my foot gets caught in its chord. I pull it back and my left leg falls out at the hip. It lands halfway inside the closet, still slightly bent. I stand it upright and place it behind the vacuum, next to the broom and dustpan.

I take out the bottle of laundry detergent, leaving the fingers and hand exposed.

My Legs

I used them as traps. Up around his back. Down under all-night diner tables. Untangling themselves as I danced for him wearing only my husband's dress shirt.

They were the longest, steadiest part of me. So sure of themselves. So even and smooth.

"Can you see anything?"

I shook my head.

"Good." My lover pulled the knot tight at the back of my head. I was wearing my husband's tie as a blindfold. "Don't move."

I heard his knees crack as he bent down. Felt his breath hot on my ankle. He traced his tongue along my calf. Nibbled the back of my knee. He ran his teeth up the inside of my thigh. "Don't you dare move."

I separate my husband's dirty clothes. I toss the darks in the washer, put the lights on top of the dryer and drop the whites onto the laundry room floor. I pour in the liquid detergent and turn the dial to the right. The machine rattles. First softly, then loudly. Violently. The walls vibrate. The air is warm and clean.

I rest against the rumbling machine and close my eyes. I run my fingers along my scalp. My hair falls out in chunks. Lands on the closed washer. I try to gather all the shaking strands. I carry them over to the utility closet and toss them into the mop bucket. I lean against the wall as I go, and I have to make several trips back to the laundry room. I leave a trail of hair behind me, and then in front of me. When I'm done picking up the hairs and putting them in the bucket, I put the mop back on top of them. The colors blend together perfectly.

I make my way over to the wall phone. I pick up the receiver and dial my husband's office.

"Hello?"

I open my mouth. I press my cheek into the cool wall.

"Hello?"

I hang up. His dark clothes need to go into the dryer.

My Hair

I used it as bait. Dangled it in front of his face. Dragged it under his nose. Promised to keep it long for him when my husband preferred it short.

It was the most dishonest part of me. Tricky and conniving. It got tangled up in things, hid the odors, changed its shape according to the weather.

"Put your head back." He ran his soapy hands across my neck, over my chest, down my sides. Poured his shampoo into his palms and rubbed it through my hair. Made small circles on my scalp with his fingers. Massaged it through the long strands. He guided me back toward the hot water and held me under there, rinsing me clean. He grabbed my hair at the roots and pulled, dipping his face into it. "Now you smell just like me."

I fold my husband's clean clothes. They are warm and dry. I lay the shirts out on the closed dryer one at a time. I fold one empty arm across the chest, and then the other over it. Fold up the bottom third, fold down the top third, set it aside on the closed washer.

The pants are more difficult to fold with only one hand. They are too long. I pick up a pair and tuck it under my chin. I smooth it down, line up the legs. My mouth hangs open as I press the rayon against my throat. I lean over to fold the bottom third up, then the middle third to the top. I set it aside and grab another pair.

I hook the belt loops under my chin and start to line up the legs and my tongue falls out onto the laundry room floor. I finish folding this pair, and then the rest of his pants, before I pick it up. I carry it over to the utility closet. Tuck it between the folded dishrags, in front of the arm.

I return to the laundry room and lay out his socks. Matching them up is the most rewarding part.

My Tongue

I used it as a spy. Crossing his boundaries. Carrying the messages back home only to hide them again. Slipping into the dark places quietly and adeptly.

It was the most gentle part of me. Gentle and soft and timid.

"Taste this." My lover fed me pieces of pineapple with his fingers. We were laying on his mattress after a shower. He fed me piece after piece. "You chew too slowly." He kissed me as I swallowed. "I like when you do things too slowly."

He opened the damp towel and licked shapes onto my stomach, my waist, the tops of my thighs. "Just keep eating."

I hear my husband open the door. Hear him close it behind him before I can cover myself. I hope he notices the clean floors. The fresh laundry scent. So that he'll be distracted by these things and won't notice the absence of my hair, of my left side.

He steps into the laundry room. "Looks like a whole new floor out there." He smiles. "Did you call?"

I nod.

"Something wrong?"

I open my mouth. The air is cold where my tongue used to be. I shake my head.

"Good. I was worried. Thought I'd come check on you." He reaches for my hand. "How about we watch some TV?" He leads me into the living room. Sits on the couch and pulls me down next to him.

He turns on the TV and lifts his socked feet onto the low table. "I can see it better from here. Thank you." When he settles on a channel, he puts the remote down and turns to me. Rests his head against the pillow behind him. "You look beautiful this afternoon." He kisses my forehead and then my cheek. Smiles at my face. "I love you."

I smile back. He nods and turns to the TV. I remember his socks. I didn't finish matching them. And it's lunch time.

I get up to go to the kitchen and my right arm falls off at the shoulder. He keeps holding the hand, rubbing it with his thumb as he watches the TV.

As she later joked to the writer Richard Gilman of calling herself Mary O'Connor: "Who was likely to buy the stories of an Irish washer-woman?" (Gooch, page 135)

The Anarchist Thinks of Winter

Christopher Kang

It bothers him to think of how many times he's been on a plane and never looked out the small window that seemed as if it were torn from an oven's door. He just appeared in a new place and felt nothing. It bothers him to think that so many are so tall and he hasn't grown since the age of fifteen. He loves but he's not so sure what he loves. There was this girl from Los Angeles that had a dog, he might have loved one of them, he's not sure. Sometimes people ask him the speci-ficities of what he believes in. And he goes on and on but barely thinks about what he says. Instead he resuscitates latent childhood memories that spring up in great detail. Walks up a steep hill in the backyard of his childhood home. At the very top of it was a tree his mother said grew peaches, but he never saw a peach. Every pet he had that died they buried under that tree. And they only had two pets, and he's not sure if either knew who he was. A rabbit, a fish. When he walked toward them, they would run away. The fish pressing against the opposite side of the tank. The rabbit darting into a bush shaped like the world. The tree split open, hollowed out, and never fell. He was twenty. His parents had disappeared. Or rather, one left and the other died. Five years apart. In between those years when one was lost and the other losing, he went up on a hot-air balloon with a friend who would later weight lift professionally. When he looked down at his own town he was unimpressed. The guilt of refusing astonishment was a new way of calibrating his defi-cient personality. He went to a therapist shortly thereafter.

The therapist said, Hello. He heard little else. It was a great success. After he was completely alone, fourteen years after, he walked into the tree and thought of death. It was a great success. He went back to the therapist and said, Hello. She said, Have we met before. He thought, Exactly. He said, No. He was in love. It was no big deal. When he thought of her, he thought of a flower. Then he thought of nothing. The flower was not as important as the nothing. The nothing was what remained. At the age of thirty-six, he moved to a town directly under the equator to help with vaccinations. When he stood outside every afternoon under the persistent sun, he cowered under the heavy line running across the sky like the shadow of a rainbow. Here this anarchist could only think of winter. It embarrassed him how every emotion was tied to snow or the cold or the bitter wind or fallen leaves or inces- sant rain. But they came in terrifying visions, as if he were seeing these landscapes reflected in a knife. One night he bought a peach, went home, and fell asleep. When he woke up the peach was beside him, sliced. He fell back asleep, and when he woke up it was gone. He went back home. He reacquainted himself. It was too easy. Don't you see, he said to a friend who just got married, don't you see that there's this thing that may or may not be the world and we are in it, and what we do next isn't meaningful but what's done next to us might be. His friend said, Okay, then disappeared with some girl from France to France. He stood at the departure gate of the airport and waved in three-fourths time and said, Goodbye. He bought a hot dog and ate it beside a baggage handler who was eating a hot dog. They could have been friends. Very good ones too. He went home. He had never been to France. He wasn't so bad, this guy. This anarchist. When he turns sixty he gets a letter that says, Hello, you don't know me but I'm your sister, and I would like to meet you.

The Cy Twombly Poem

It's extremely arduous to grasp your second-tier status as an interesting human being while trying to figure out why the hell you're in love with a Good Friend who doesn't like to go to the beach. These realizations parade past me in reluctant processions while in front of this Cy Twombly painting in Philadelphia when suddenly my phone goes off and I pick it up because no one else is in the room, it's just me and these six massive paintings based loosely on the Trojan War, and, hey, it's my Good Friend and she's at the beach. She says, I'm at the beach, can you believe it, oh my god, I'm at the beach. And I laugh ceremoniously like a twenty one gun salute although I am terrified by this news, as I always felt the essential part of who she was relied upon her reluctance to go to the beach. Is the water warm, I say, is it nice, are the waves coming in big and steady, are you riding on a wave right now, tell me all about it you deceitful bitch. What is wrong with you, she says, where are you now, what's *wrong* with you? I'm at the beach too, I say, the water is warm, it's nice, the waves are coming in big and steady, I'm riding one right now, it's taking me away, it's taking me to you right now, and I couldn't be happier. An annoyed silence. One, two, three, four, five, six, seven, eight, nine, ten, eleven, twelve, thirteen, fourteen, fifteen, sixteen, seventeen, eighteen, nineteen, twenty, twenty-one, why doesn't she hang up? You liar, she finally says. You stupid, ugly liar, she says softer now, as if her lungs are deflating. You're right, no, you're absolutely right, I'm not on a wave, I'm actually reclined sideways on a gigantic, plush velvet pillow in a recently inherited mansion perched on the ambient low-lying hills of Tennessee, the pillow's dimensions are exactly the same as your childhood home's front lawn, where we first kissed, and it feels as soft as the folds of fat on your arm that I liked to jiggle when you were fast asleep, it never woke you up, and I'll be honest, that always surprised me. She snored in ellipses, and I loved her for it, go figure. I want to hang up, she says, but something is holding me back, what is it? I was wondering that same thing, I say. Another silence that takes on a spherical shape the more we let it sit. I could never kiss you again, she says, and it has nothing to do with your face, it has something to do with an immoveable compartment of incompatibility that you'll always treasure and I'll always have to endure, so stop wishing, I'm tired of being in all those imagined places and in all those pathetically choreographed situations in your fat head. I'm crying my eyes out, I say. Sometimes I wish I could shift the world in its vulnerable places, I wish I could puncture the emotional pockets that fortify my wounded identity, but I can't, I just can't. You know, sometimes I stand at the edge of a staircase and think that it's just too much. The careful organization of this architectural feature just so I can get where I'm trying to go. It kills me. The worst is when they construct a staircase that winds around a mountain like those Florida snakes that wrap around their prey to suffocate it into submission. Things will always be tall, but I don't need to be anywhere close to their summit. I'm just fine staying very still and close to the ground, thank you very much. But still, but still I manage to suffocate. See, she was always busy composing seven-hour operas filled with characters based on everyone but me, and she would ask me what I thought of them. What was I supposed to say? Too often she went off to a dance party while I stood in front of a fan, my back to an enormous television breathlessly preaching something about the evolution of the modern day bullet. You realize you're narrating out loud, she says, you can be a real moron sometimes, you know that, a real *doofus*. Buhh, I say. I have written arias about you, she says, they were never very good, and I wanted them to be good, honest, but when I put your songs in the sopranos' mouths by the final note they always end up dying, violently, erupting guts and blood and hard candy and everything on the poor percussionist in the pit, and I'm sorry, I'm *sorry* if that hurts you because sometimes I too feel enraged by a staircase wrapping around a colossal triangle shaped mountain piercing a fat cloud. Uh oh, I say. My train leaves in an hour, taking me just a little bit further away from her, a little bit closer to home, and I realize how frequently I've been waiting these past few years. These thoughts I keep firmly to myself, I know she doesn't hear a word of it. I verify this because the entire meticulous procedure of hermetically sealing rogue thoughts leaves me a little wounded. Well, she says impatiently. I stare at a painting that looks like a projection of Achilles's whispering laughter as he bleeds in extraordinary rhythms. It fills me with a cartoonish courage. One, two, three, four, wait, wait, okay now. I'm not riding on a wave, I say, nor am I even remotely close to a pillow of any size, but I am being taken away from you, right now, like a cube-shaped kite swept into the formless, endless sky, and from this height although I can see everything I close my eyes and choose to imagine you. I'm not at a beach, she says, interrupting me. I'm right behind you, she says, turn around for Chrissake so I can kill you.

Strawberry once saw Rodney Bingenheimer alone in a booth at Canter's and looked away. (Saroyan, page 73)

Las Vegas Bypass

Benjamin Golliver

I.

PULLING OFF TO THE SIDE OF THE CURVING ROAD TO TAKE IN the Hoover Dam is a great way to forget that today's high temperature was 106 degrees. It's 8:30 p.m., and it's still pushing ninety outside, and there's a slight breeze coming in over the orange hills above, so that the shirt I'm wearing unsticks itself from uncomfortable skin as a digital camera snaps. The dam, concrete upon concrete, stretches as far as the eye can see, in all directions, provoking all sorts of questions from nearby tourists, none more common than, "Where's all the water?" The canyon walls are marked white by decades of current flow but today the actual water line is at least fifty feet below the white marks. Can an entire river evaporate?

The ride from McCarran Airport to the dam was pleasant and quick, a thirty-mile burst through the desert, pickups with gargantuan off-road tires kicking up dust alongside us. "I always slow down going through Boulder City," says my travel companion as we approach the dam. "The cops here are pretty ambitious." It appears that they are quite successful, too; seconds later, I spot a shiny red SUV with BCPD tattooed on the side pulling out of a driveway, sirens blaring in hot pursuit of a minivan that must have, somehow, exceeded the posted thirty miles per hour speed limit. Boulder City police, and the citizens they protect, don't have many concerns. The small town, with a perfect view of Lake Mead, is dotted with million-dollar residences. It wasn't always this way.

II.

Smoking crack, apparently, is a great way to forget that today's high temperature was 106 degrees. It's 1 a.m., it's still almost ninety degrees, and there is heavy foot traffic in all directions along Swenson and Twain. It's a people potpourri, yes; hookers, tourists, swing-shifters, partygoers, cops, and, of course, corner boys and their customers.

The corner boys here sell it all, or so I am told. "Meth for white people, rock for blacks, but everyone seems to agree on one thing," says my travel companion, "the quality of drugs here is shit." I nod, taking in this information slowly, my eyes peeled to three o'clock where two LVPD squad cars have pulled into a gas station, sirens blaring as Young Black Men drop instinctively to their knees, hands in the air, the universal code for "I'm not resisting, please don't shoot." Earlier today, at this same gas station, I saw a woman beating the heat by not wearing any pants. The oversized T-shirt as dress look had been in full effect. She looked like a hurricane evacuee but there was no hurricane. I had tried to laugh it off. I had tried to forget about her.

I look across the street to a concrete strip of check-cashing places and convenience stores and I lock the car doors. We are waiting at a stop light, just trying to get home. At this moment, this isn't where I want to be. It wasn't always this way.

III.

Watching Jerryd Bayless's cesarean section entry into the National Basketball Association is a great way to forget that today's high temperature was 106 degrees. It's about 7 p.m., and it's a cool seventy-two degrees inside the Thomas and Mack gym, and the crowd of thousands is hyped up. Jerryd Bayless cannot be stopped.

Jerryd is the newest Portland Trail Blazer, type A from head to toe: precise haircut, precise wardrobe, precise movement. When he steps into the gym, he glares. When he warms up, he glares. When he cuts to the basket, his body glares at the defense, offended by their weak attempts to stop his advances. When he jumps, his body glares at gravity. He is the best player on the court and he knows it. He glares to let you know that he knows it.

The impact of his entry into the minds of the assembled basketball intelligentsia is forceful and it levitates in the gym air. Ooh. Aah. Scouts, coaches, and general managers are not an excitable bunch, especially not in Las Vegas in July. Usually, they can be picked out of the crowd because they do not react to spectacular plays and they furiously jot notes when the casual observer might wonder, "Did I just miss something?" But the bounce to Jerryd's swag is very real, his dribble is emphatic and effortless, his body control borders on mind control. He is drawing new maps to the basket, he is absorbing contact, and he is brushing his shoulder off. Everyone is taking note. Even the scouts are smirking, which is as close as they get to smiling. Jerryd's parents, both his mother and his father, cheer him on; Jerryd is the younger son, his brother works on Wall Street. An investment banker and a professional basketball player, they couldn't be prouder. One suspects that, in lighter circumstances, his parents get to see a nice young man behind the glare.

His coach for the summer, Monty Williams, former professional player, tall, dark, handsome, bald, still in game shape, stands courtside, arms folded, watching along with the rest of us. Bayless hits an impossible game winner. The gym erupts. It feels like playoff basketball in early June for a moment, not Summer League in the middle of July. Monty, a deep-thinking devout Christian, is old enough to have enjoyed last-second wins before but still young enough to get excited by the thrill of that moment, the pulse of victory. Dressed in his red coach's polo shirt, Monty wipes his brow, trying hard to contain a big smile. He is at ease.

His boss, Blazers head coach, Nate McMillan, former professional player, tall, dark, handsome, bald, not quite in game shape anymore, makes his way down from high in the stands, looking comfortable and serene, but not overjoyed. This is just another buzzer beater for Nate, one of hundreds if not thousands that he has seen in his lifetime. Nate doesn't allow himself to display happiness. Nate knows basketball and he appreciates great shots. Below the hardened exterior, he's probably ecstatic. It wasn't always this way.

IV.

In recent years, Las Vegas Police groups have resisted efforts to track traffic stops by ethnicity and age, a measure proposed by Nevada legislators in an effort to cut down on rampant racial profiling. Las Vegas and Nevada, underneath the mafia legends and strip club debauchery, still have a very real problem with race. How many remember that Las Vegas was once known as the "Little Mississippi of the West?" How many know that corrections officers at the High Desert State Prison recently stated that prisoners were being segregated on the basis of race? How many know that in October 2007, just a few hundred miles from Vegas, Esmeralda County school district officials approved a policy that prohibited Spanish from being spoken on school buses?

Riding shotgun at 1 a.m. I didn't know. I had no idea. When I thought of Las Vegas, I thought of lobsters in Hawaiian shirts gambling away their childrens' college savings. I thought of standing in line after line at trendy nightclubs and overpriced shows. I thought of conventioneers with colored name tags. I thought of never-ending marketing: what happens here stays here. I thought of idyllic poolside pictures on Facebook. I thought of middle class white America. I thought of escape.

Riding shotgun at 1 a.m., I thought different things. I looked out the car window and saw a figure darting across the street corner in front of us and thought, "Something isn't quite right with that boy."

He was, to my best guess, seventeen years old, his jean shorts almost prototypically baggy, hanging to his ankles, his bright white high-tops visibly shiny even at this late hour. He crossed the street from our right to left, his demeanor paranoid. He kept looking back at the gas station, at the cops, and, I assumed, at his friends who were still kneeling. As he neared the sidewalk he cut the corner heading west, stepping outside the marked pedestrian walkway in a manner seen on every Manhattan street corner one million times a day. He stood no more than fifteen feet away from our car. In a flash visible in his eye, those brief, horrifying seconds of recognition, two rollers were on him, screeching to a stop just behind us, doors flying open, guns drawn. His motion ceased, stunned, as a cop approached, grabbing him by the cuff, detaining him. My eyes must have look confused. "Jaywalking," my travel companion explained. "It's the perfect excuse."

I didn't see anything else. The light turned green and we continued through the intersection.

V.

The Hoover Dam was built during the Great Depression, the last time the American economy was this bad. This humongous public works project to redirect the Colorado River was seen as a beacon for destitute folk across the country. Thousands migrated to the desert in hopes of employment. It was arduous work and the struggles that went into creating the dam remain a part of local lore to this day. The shantytown in which many workers lived, dubbed "Ragtown," was straight out of Thomas Hobbes, unbearably hot during summer, unbearably cold during winter. But, you are apt to hear the story told, "The Hoover Dam was completed two full years ahead of schedule." And this is true.

It is only partly true, though, because as bad as things might have been for whites working at the Hoover Dam site, conditions were significantly worse for blacks. Life and workplace were fully segregated. Blacks were not allowed to live in the mythic Ragtown and were excluded from Boulder City entirely. With no other choice, they made a long commute from Las Vegas each day. Once on site, they were forced to drink from separate water sources and work in the heat of the Arizona gravel pits. Given the economic conditions, they had no alternative.

Viewing the dam last week I didn't see any of this. I took my digital pictures, hopped back in the car and returned to Las Vegas.

VI.

The Las Vegas Summer League, conceived in recent years as a showcase for draft picks, international players, and other professionals trying to make an NBA roster, is both a tremendous opportunity and a graveyard for the hopes and dreams of the nearly good-enoughs. The off court scene is breathtaking: Hall of Famers, owners, general managers, scouts, national media personalities, and fans, black and white, mingle harmoniously. It is the one place that diehards with foam fingers can backslap with the millionaires, or billionaires, that run their favorite team. Even the stodgiest basketball executives seem to agree that this is healthy for everyone.

On the court there is no harmony. There are players who have spots assured. They loaf. There are players who need their names printed on the back of their jerseys, otherwise no one would know who they are. There is a young man, O.J. Mayo, looking to make a highlight film; there is another, Nick Young, looking at the fly honeys. There is a mountain man, Steven Hill, whose beard inspires more cheers than his play; there is a play the game the right way plodder, Josh Davis, who has every white scout over sixty years old wishing him the best.

Importantly, the racial divide between the players and the fans that exists in many places does not exist here. The racial divide that seems to exist everywhere else in this city—the ancient divide between the haves and the have-nots—is replaced by a different, more meritocratic divide: can he ball?

"How is he playing?" I hear this a lot from new friends and strangers, curious to know the fate of an otherwise-forgotten career or an unproven up-and-comer. I soak this up as the gym empties, leaving only a few of my fellow writers pecking away at keyboards. I wanted to stay all night but, at the same time, I wanted to get out of there immediately.

VII.

In 2005, the Hoover Dam Bypass project was undertaken to alleviate heavy traffic that is caused by the many switchbacks that lead to the Hoover Dam. The bypass will ensure uninterrupted traffic along Highway 93, a NAFTA route. Expected to be completed in 2010, it will consist of a two thousand foot long bridge that crosses the Colorado River, spanning a mountain gap between Nevada and Arizona.

Looking at an unfinished bridge sitting high above a nearly empty dam, one formidable engineering project piled on top of another, a new route literally, intentionally, bypassing American history, I watch that history evaporate with the water. I imagine international commerce proceeding more efficiently and I take heart knowing that less will be sacrificed during the construction process this time around.

But I can't help but look down and wonder where all the water went. If the Dam ends up completely empty one day will the exposed riverbed tell the old stories? Probably not. Will people look down from the bridge and wonder?

VIII.

The narcotics arrest I witnessed is now available as a data point in the Las Vegas Police Department's Crime View online service, which tracks incidents citywide. In the week since the boy jaywalked at Swenson and Twain, there were a number of calls for police assistance at that very same corner: a report of a stolen vehicle, an assault with a deadly weapon, and others.

It had been just another night, just another arrest, just another data point at the corner of Swenson and Twain.

There is no glamour in this scene. Those living nearby, including my travel companion, are resigned to the reality. In a divided city, and country, I see the Thomas and Mack as a bypass from the thousands of corners like Swenson and Twain. As an outsider wishing for more than the false security of a locked car, the thought of the gym, that artificial enclave, is comforting. I want that bypass. Take me there. Anywhere. Out of here. Go.

IX.

The last Sunday of Summer League is an afterthought. The refs have traded in the quick whistle for the let 'em play; the coaches have traded in micromanaging for air it out; even the players who are looking to make a roster realize that their fates have probably already been sealed.

After the final game, another last-second win, Monty Williams looks relieved. His broad shoulders relax. Summer League is a hectic time for a young coach. Monty pulled off a winning record and although Summer League records are supposedly meaningless this seemed to mean something to him.

His boss, Nate McMillan, now prepares to check out of the luxury hotel he was staying in as coach of the Trail Blazers. He will cross the street and check into a luxury hotel that he will be staying in as an assistant coach for the United States Men's National Basketball Team, which is in final preparations for the 2008 Beijing Olympics. Coach McMillan, the only African-American coach on Team USA's coaching staff, has recently admitted in interviews that he is tired, that he can't wait until the next off-season so that he will finally have time for a much-needed vacation.

The obvious pressure to perform as a coach, the underlying pressure to serve as a pillar of a city, the forgotten pressure of having succeeded against a stacked deck, to an observer, is unimaginable. To do it despite the fatigue, with the eyes of younger black men like Monty Williams and Jerryd Bayless trained upon him, is grace bigger than any basketball court.

X.

For professional basketball players, particularly the best players in the game, one heart is simply not enough. There are more tattoos of hearts on NBA bodies than there are NBA bodies. As the game has integrated and globalized, heart has emerged as the defining measure of a basketball player's worth. Does he possess the ability to perform phenomenal acts under extreme pressure? If so, a player is clutch with ice water in his veins. If not, the player is a choker   his heart pumps Kool-Aid. Stars talk serenely about finding a zone, where their pulse slows down and the rest of the world hesitates just long enough for a path to victory to unveil itself. After big plays, whether in the NBA or on the playground, it's not uncommon to see a player pull at his jersey and bang his exposed chest, as if to say, "See, I told you I had heart. It's right here. Look at it." Often, this is accompanied by a glare.

Some months before Summer League, I sought out Monty Williams because I had read that while in college at Notre Dame, he had over-come a strange heart condition. I was recovering from open- heart surgery at the time and was looking for inspiration or diversion or conversation—all of the above, I guess.

Heart surgery had broken me down. I had wrapped my head around what it would mean to be dead at twenty-four. I had reminded myself constantly that the risks of the procedure were relatively min-imal. I had pictured my chest pried open with people looking down into it. It's the kind of trauma that I avoid talking about at all costs. It's easier to just move on and pretend it didn't happen, even if the scar stares back in the mirror every morning. But it's also the kind of trau-ma that makes my ears perk up if I find out someone is similarly afflicted.

Monty told me that when he found out about his heart condition in 1990, at age nineteen, he was forced to come to terms with the fact that his career was over. Doctors couldn't fully explain the condition so they couldn't in good conscience let him continue playing. "We prayed, went to church, prayed some more, the church elders laid hands on me," he told me. Then he waited.

Almost two years later Monty's symptoms completely disappeared. Again, the doctors had no answers for him. He told me that his unexpected recovery was an act of God, unexplainable by science. "A miracle, there's nothing else to call it," he said, looking directly into my eyes, as serious as a person can be.

The doctors agreed to let him return to the court but the mysterious condition had tarnished his reputation, costing him millions of dollars as team after team passed him by in the NBA draft. And, in those days, there was no Summer League to help jumpstart a career. He put his head down, listened and learned from his veteran teammates, paid attention to details, and became a serviceable role player. He went into coaching immediately after retiring as a player. Those two years spent away from the game during college had been enough.

By chance, Monty and I were on the same Sunday night flight out of Las Vegas. As I passed by his seat in first class, I smiled broadly and offered a fist-pound, both of which Monty returned graciously. I attempted to joke, "You know, I'm going to have to interview you about your thoughts on this flight." Monty laughed a short, easy laugh, and quickly said, "I'm off the clock."

"You earned it, coach," I mumbled to myself as I shuffled down the aisle looking for my seat. Stretched out comfortably, with the winning Summer League record, with a young roster that is the toast of the league, and with home in Portland just a two hour flight away, the last thing Monty needed, from me or anyone else, was validation. For Monty, there had been raw ability, hard work, luck, and, in his mind, the grace of God. In his ten year playing career and three seasons as an assistant coach, there had been a lot of heart. There had not been any shortcuts or end-arounds. There was no bypass.

Recipient

Jennifer Kronovet

There was a time when she was less
a concept; each body is less ash
than thought. Away was *away*
like California or Alaska.
Now, nevermind.

Feeling harder does earn you
a prize: a new shape named
for you in the world of shapes
where no one lives.

You are more mother, and I
am a partially collapsible line
named Jenny.

A Self-Guided Tour

The "Room for Listening to Rain"
was difficult to locate, but we found it
on the small hill. It wasn't raining
but we heard it, pretended
to hear it, heard its history
as one hears through wood. Wood
that was taken from a shrine
to build a temple, then taken from
the temple to build her house.
We could hear that house—
the sorry/not sorry hum of it.
Under the sound of rain together
because the roof was low and country,
knowing the exact size of not knowing
you. You, through night, then through me.
"She died of illness after all measures
to resuscitate her had been applied."
"She was skilled in German and English."

Together

Here, at eighteen one must choose to have a bed for dreaming in or a bed for making love in. You think that this would be an easy choice. The sun has set but there is light that makes the country classically itself. If this were before, you would have longed for someone unknown to you. But this person is here, telling you about the first time he realized someone might not like him. She was a nun, and he was a child.

The first years without dreams, you don't know if you've slept. And then you know you have. And then you know you haven't.

One summer you purposefully stay awake together to imagine the forest inhabited by animals drawn by everyone in the country. You choose your words to make it more real, irritated by slips into the easily known. Be specific about how the deer run. How much of it is graceful and how much of it the violent jerk of fear, or of thoughtlessness.

We're doing it Lewis and Clark, they'd say, We're doing it no maps. (Spain, page 33)

Flannery at Iowa

Brad Gooch

SITTING IN HIS OFFICE EARLY IN THE FALL OF 1945, PAUL ENGLE, the director of the Iowa Writers' Workshop, heard a gentle knock at the door. After he shouted an invitation to enter, a shy, young woman appeared and walked over to his desk without, at first, saying a word. He could not even tell, as she stood before him, whether she was looking in his direction, or out the window at the curling Iowa River below. A hulking six foot four inch poet, in his thirties, with wavy dark hair, alert blue eyes, and expressive eyebrows, Engle quickly took the lead. He introduced himself and offered her a seat, as she tightly held on to what he later claimed was "one of the most beat-up handbags I've ever seen."

When she finally spoke, her Georgia dialect sounded so thick to his Midwestern ear that he asked her to repeat her question. Embarrassed by an inability a second time, to understand, Engle handed her a pad to write what she had said. So in schoolgirl script, she put down three short lines: "My name is Flannery O'Connor. I am not a journalist. Can I come to the Writers' Workshop?" Engle suggested that she drop off writing samples, and they would consider her, late as it was. The next day a few stories arrived, and to his near disbelief, he found them to be "imaginative, tough, alive." She was instantly accepted to the Workshop, both the name of Engle's writing class and of his MFA graduate writing program, the first in the nation, to which she would switch her affiliation from the Graduate School of Journalism by the second semester.

For all of her outward timidity, she had quickly found her way to Engle, and her vocation. Just a few weeks earlier, the third week in September, she and her mother had departed Milledgeville together. In Atlanta, they boarded a train to Chicago, where they transferred at La Salle Street Station. They then made the four hour trip west to Iowa City on the Rock Island Railroad, through a countryside of cornfields, apple orchards, and colts grazing on grassy hillocks. Anticipating subzero winters, O'Connor arrived carrying a fifteen-pound muskrat coat. Mrs. O'Connor stayed long enough to make sure that her only child was comfortably settled in Currier House, at 32 East Bloomington Street, a two-story, old brick, corner building, housing fifteen or twenty graduate women in double rooms.

Iowa City was a nearly rural university town of about eighteen thousand year-round residents. Downtown consisted of four or five banks, a couple of hotels, as well as drugstores, bookshops, tea rooms, and beer halls rigged for student trade. Like Milledgeville, this Johnson County seat had once been the state capital, until the government moved to Des Moines in 1855. Left behind was the gold-domed Old Capitol, revamped as the State University of Iowa main administration building, set high on a hill in the center of town, near a Masonic Temple. Quiet residential backstreets were lined with dull clapboard houses, interspersed with some Victorian follies. O'Connor later told Robert Lowell that she quickly responded to the "naturally blank" tenor of the place: "I always liked it in spite of those sooty tubercular-looking houses."

In September 1945, more than 11,600 students enrolled for the fall term, expanding the town's population by more than half, and helping to bolster its extravagant nickname, "The Athens of the Midwest." With the highest percentage of full-time, resident PhDs in the country, town-gown friction was not a problem. The 425-acre campus was viewed more as an extension of the city, like a municipal park sloping down from the Old Capitol to sturdy footbridges spanning the muddy Iowa River. Its nine colleges, housed in fifty-odd gray stone buildings, on both the east and west banks of the bisecting river, introduced into the life of the city each fall aspiring doctors, dentists, lawyers, engineers, businessmen, actors, musicians, writers, and artists. The Iowa Hawkeyes, a Big Ten college football team, generated alarming civic frenzy at home games in the monumental Iowa Stadium.

This influx was greatly exaggerated in 1945 by a spike in enrollment from returning veterans, increasing through the spring and peaking in the fall of 1946. In the wake of the formal surrender of the Japanese to General Douglas MacArthur, on September 2, marking the end of World War II, millions of demobilized soldiers started streaming back from Europe and the Pacific. A large number took advantage of the GI Bill of Rights, or Servicemen's Readjustment Act of 1944, providing a free college education and one year of unemployment compensation. "Iowa City was a bustling place," recalls one graduate, "because it was flooded with GI Bill students, as well as droves of foreign exchange students."

To returning vets, with more worldly experience, the county seat, its feeder roads crowded with trucks full of pigs, could look ominously "hick." Many had been in the position of Haze Motes, in O'Connor's novel *Wise Blood*, which she began in the Workshop the next year: "The army sent him halfway around the world and forgot him." Yet as John Sullivan was moved by wartime experiences to study for the priesthood, others resolved to lead creative lives: they wanted to write the great American novel, play jazz, or paint. To their relief, they soon discovered a homegrown artistic tradition of "regionalism," as exemplified in *American Gothic*, the iconic portrait of a stately farmer, with pitchfork, and his wife, painted in the thirties by the faculty member Grant Wood. Arriving to sign up for the Workshop in midsemester the next spring, still in his "Eisenhower jacket" and parachute jump boots, James B. Hall wrote of "a new Bohemia, albeit in cornfields."

Yet no amount of prairie-flower bohemianism, or postwar

euphoria, could assuage O'Connor's first reaction to her new surroundings: homesickness. Far from her extended family, and speaking a dialect routinely treated as a foreign language, she experienced an acute ache. As she later wrote to her friend Maryat Lee, of "The Geranium," her first published Iowa story, "I did know what it meant to be homesick." At Currier House, she roomed with a couple of rumba-loving suitemates who cranked up the volume on the record player. While remaining friendly toward them, she soon relished their weekend departures. Every day she wrote a letter to her mother, who wrote back daily replies, as well as forwarding the weekly Milledgeville newspaper.

Her home away from home did not turn out to be Currier House—and certainly not the Airliner, a long, narrow tavern, just across from campus, with white tile floors and a jukebox, popular with other students. Instead she found the antidote for her homesickness two blocks away at St. Mary's Catholic Church, on East Jefferson Street. A modest, brick structure with a clock-tower steeple, built in 1869, St. Mary's provided a worship experience enriched by seventeen church bells. Its high altar was crowded with Victorian paintings and pastel statues of St. Patrick and St. Boniface, reflecting the mixed demographic of Irish and Germans in the parish. In the fall of 1945, the church pastor, Monsignor Carl Bernstein, offered daily morning masses at six thirty and seven thirty. As O'Connor told Roslyn Barnes, a young woman enrolled in the Workshop, in 1960, "I went to St. Mary's as it was right around the corner and I could get there practically every morning. I went there three years and never knew a soul in that congregation or any of the priests, but it was not necessary. As soon as I went in the door I was at home."

With the same deliberation that she applied to coming up with her "MFOC" monogram signature for her first college cartoon, and a revised name, "M. F. O'Connor," for her first published college story, she decided nearly from day one at Iowa to introduce herself, and to sign her papers, as "Flannery O'Connor." Everyone who met her in Iowa City knew her simply as "Flannery." Yet unlike her character Joy, who spitefully changed her name to Hulga when she went away to college in the story "Good Country People," O'Connor asked her mother's permission in advance. Partly she wanted to lose the lilting double name that exaggerated her oddity as a Southern lady in Iowa City, but she also looked forward to her byline when she fulfilled a wish to write what Engle said she described to him as "shom stor-rowies." As she later joked to the writer Richard Gilman of calling herself Mary O'Connor: "Who was likely to buy the stories of an Irish washerwoman?"

Enrolled for the fall semester in the Graduate School of Journalism, Flannery had a course load that was tilted, at first, in the direction of magazine work. She took Magazine Writing, with William Porter, a mustached pulp-fiction writer, given to wearing rumpled checked shirts, who had sold a couple of crime stories to the movies. He geared his course to "selling stories to magazines." O'Connor wrote for Porter her short, somewhat flat-footed "Biography." In Principles of Advertising, with Mr. Gordon, she studied commercial art. Her single political-science course, American Political Ideas, was a survey of "representative American thinkers" from Roger Williams to James Madison, including a discussion of political cartooning. She received a grade of B in all three courses.

Still holding out for a possible career as a cartoonist, Flannery submitted cartoons and drawings to the art department to be admitted to the two-semester course Advanced Drawing, and to Individual Instruction. Hoping for some extra income, she submitted her cartoons to trade journals, expecting the competition would not be as steep as at *The New Yorker*, but with no success. As the art building was located on the west campus, she would walk to her life-drawing classes over a bridge, just below the Iowa Memorial Union and along gravel paths crowded with familiar enough companions—flocks of mud-caked geese. The department was lively during that era: the artist Philip Guston, an associate professor, won first prize in a Carnegie Institute "Painting in the United States, 1945" show; Mauricio Lasansky was setting up a world-class print studio.

Yet by knocking at the door of Paul Engle that fall afternoon, O'Connor had begun to shift her direction away from art toward what was called "imaginative writing" at Iowa. He immediately enrolled her in two of his classes, Understanding Fiction and Writers' Workshop (the double-listed Workshop was credited as "Journalism" in her fall semester, and as "English" afterward). Engle was the one-man band of the Workshop. During the war years, it had been simply an informal class with eight or ten students. Earning one of the first creative graduate degrees in America, at Iowa, in 1932, for his collection of poems, *Worn Earth*, published in the prestigious Yale Series of Younger Poets, Engle became a tireless champion of the MFA concept. As he liked to brag of his program, "You can get an M.A. degree without counting the commas in Shakespeare."

The title of his lit course was actually the title of its textbook, an anthology of stories that O'Connor later said Engle "was able to breathe some life into"—*Understanding Fiction*. Published in 1943, it had been edited by Cleanth Brooks, Jr. and Robert Penn Warren, with interspersed explanations. An academic marker for the fashionable school of New Criticism, its editors emphasized "close reading," paying attention to the art and craft of stories, rather than to historical or cultural concerns, or to mining fiction for a series of psychological clues to a writer's life. Many of the selections were eye-openers for Flannery: Caroline Gordon's "Old Red"; Guy de Maupassant's "The Necklace"; Nathaniel Hawthorne's "The Birthmark"; William Faulkner's "A Rose for Emily." In an exam essay in November, she argued that Thomas Thompson's "A Shore for the Sinking" was about "a man's realization that he has been 'left out.'" Engle wrote on her blue book, "A+. Admirable."

All of the creative writers at Iowa, and many painters and musicians, too, passed through Engle's Workshop. Still in its nascent wartime stage in the fall of 1945, the writing seminar was taught in the English department faculty offices, or in a small classroom in the University building, next to the Old Capitol on the Pentacrest of five buildings. "It was a plain little room in an old building on campus that nobody was competing for," recalls one student. A dozen chairs would simply be drawn into an informal semicircle around a reading desk set on a platform a wooden step up from the floor. As Paul Engle described the class routine in the *Des Moines Register*, "Each meeting consists of the reading of manuscripts by, customarily, two students... The students are quite merciless in criticizing each other's work, as well as in challenging the faculty before them."

One of a small minority of women in the 1945 Workshop, Mary Mudge Wiatt, from Sioux City, was present the first time Flannery read a story. "Her voice was quiet, with a nice, rich Southern accent," remembers Wiatt. "I thought she seemed not really at ease. She colored easily, flushed. I remember one scene where a white woman answers the door. A black man had some business with her. They spoke back and forth." The story, a draft of "The Coat," was Flannery's attempt to mimic a selection she admired in her *Understanding Fiction* anthology, "The Necklace," by Maupassant. In the original French moral tale, a string of paste jewels, mistaken for diamonds, destroys the heroine's life. In her Southern rewrite, Rosa, a black washerwoman, invites tragedy on her husband, Abram, by wrongly imagining that he killed a white man for "dat coat."

O'Connor wrote about this shaky period in Iowa, trying to find her way as a writer, for the *Alumnae Journal* at Georgia State College for Women, when the magazine was running a series on choices in career paths. In a piece titled "The Writer and the Graduate School," which appeared in the summer of 1948, she confessed her initial doubts: "What first stuns the young writer emerging from college is that there is no clear-cut road for him to travel on. He must chop a path in the wilderness of his own soul; a disheartening process, lifelong and lonesome. Therefore, of what use graduate work?" She answered her own question, with some of her arch high school humor, by claiming that a creative writing program at least saved a few authentic writers from becoming one of the scholarly "dead birds" in "the literary woods": "Some of these were laid away with PhD's and doubtless all with an excellent knowledge of Beowulf." The

MFA program was an alternative, she concluded, to "the poor house" and "the mad house."

An early boost came with a classroom visit from the poet John Crowe Ransom, the founder and editor of the *Kenyon Review*, the house organ of the New Critics. Visits from such writers deemed, by Engle, "of the right sort," were an important component of the Workshop. When Ransom chose one of O'Connor's stories to read to the class, she was encouraged to be singled out, and by such a prominent Southern writer. Yet the work was in the mode of her high school story "A Place of Action," or "The Coat." She was trying to render the dialogue of poor whites and blacks in the South. When Ransom came across the word "nigger," he refused to read it aloud, substituting the word "Negro." "It did spoil the story," Flannery complained to Robie Macauley, after he arrived as a Workshop instructor in 1947. "The people I was writing about would never use any other word."

For one of her next stories, she turned again to *Understanding Fiction*, and Caroline Gordon's "Old Red," for a model. By now, winter had dramatically fallen on Iowa City. Flannery had been home to Georgia for the Christmas holidays and discovered that she had grown more than an inch her first semester, up to about five five. By the time she returned for the February 3 resumption of classes, the cornfields were a silent blur of thick, fallen snow. Fellow Workshop member Norma Hodges recalls walking out after one evening Workshop meeting into the bracing Iowa air: "Flannery was so cold, she was shivering all over. I said something about, 'Not quite your Southern weather.'" Always tense around the "little pale girl with big glasses," Hodges felt her silly pleasantry returned with "one of those dirty, dirty looks. I didn't mess with her much."

Yet on the day Flannery read her "Old Red"–inspired story, Hodges was "flabbergasted. I was real excited about Flannery when I heard her. But then the men gave her a hard time, which seemed funny." The story she read was a draft of "The Geranium." In Gordon's "Old Red," an old Southern gentleman finds a symbol for his life in a wily red fox. In O'Connor's story, a Southerner, Old Dudley, living in a tenement in New York City, finds a symbol for his homesickness in a potted red geranium. As she later wrote to Maryat Lee of this story, expressing the underlying emotion of her first winter in Iowa City, "I couldn't though have written a story about *my* being homesick." Instead she embodied the experience in "an old man who went to live in a New York slum—no experience of mine as far as old men and slums went."

The early mimeographed draft Flannery read in a contentious Workshop session had a more extreme ending that was later cut. Upon finding that the pot had fallen off a windowsill, the old man, rather than merely feeling crushed, as in the final version, according to Hodges, "pitched himself out of the window. I think his daughter asked, 'Where are you going?' and Old Dudley said, 'After that damned geranium!'" But feelings among the men in the class were already stacked against O'Connor as she began reading the story with what Hodges called a "broad Southern drawl": "After a few lines, groans arose from the oval of chairs and the story was given to a man with more recognizable diction." When the old man leapt to his death—a finale Hodges found "mythical"—"They all went, 'No . . . couldn't happen . . . it's too much,' and so on."

"The only day I felt she fell flat on her face was when she tried to write about a boy-and-girl situation," Hodges added, of O'Connor's talent for these "mythical" stories. "It wasn't her thing. And one about an educated black became labored." Engle likewise noted her awkwardness in writing about sex or romance. In the corridor, following one Workshop session, he tried to make a few suggestions. "'This scene of the attempted seduction just is not correct, I want to explain,'" he said. "'Oh no, don't, not here!'" Flannery quickly replied, looking nervously about. "'So we went outside, across the street to the parking lot and into my car. There, I explained to her that sexual seduction didn't take place quite the way she had written it—I suspect from a lovely lack of knowledge.'"

If Engle felt that her sex scenes were not graphic enough, Flannery was still worried about their mere existence in the work of a young Catholic writer. As she later wrote of this crisis of literary conscience, "I was right young and very ignorant and I thought what I was doing was mighty powerful (it wasn't even intelligible at that point) and liable to corrupt anybody that read it and me too." Her solution was to visit one of the local Iowa City priests and carefully explain the problem. The priest drew out from his stash "one of those ten cent pamphlets that they are never without" and told her that she didn't need to write for fifteen-year-old girls. While this permission to write for a wider adult audience was helpful, his pamphlet failed to impress when she discovered that its Jesuit author deemed *A Tree Grows in Brooklyn* "about as good as you could get."

O'Connor later told an interviewer, concerning the Workshop, "When I went there I didn't know a short story from an ad in the newspaper." In spite of her insecurities, Engle encouraged her to keep submitting work for publication. Her first submission to the *Sewanee Review* was rejected over Christmas break. But in February, she mailed off two more stories, "The Geranium" and "The Crop," to *Accent* magazine. A broad satire in the style of some of her juvenile fiction, "The Crop" concerned a spinster schoolmarm with pretensions of becoming a writer of "social problem" stories. Like the young Miss O'Connor, trying on different author's story lines, the assiduous Miss Willerton, sitting in front of her typewriter, "discarded subject after subject and it usually took her a week or two to decide finally on something."

In March, close to her twenty-first birthday, O'Connor received word that "The Geranium" had been accepted for publication in the summer issue of *Accent*. Flannery was now "published," a crucial distinction in the Workshop. A "little magazine" from the University of Illinois, credited with printing the first stories of J. F. Powers and William Gass, *Accent* was on a short list of publications considered "of the right sort" among the Workshop members. Flannery admitted to a fellow student that she had not begun to think of herself as a fiction writer until the respected literary magazine had taken her first story, adding, "Although I reckon I got a long way to get yet before I'm what you call good at it." As she simply parsed her achievement at Iowa to the TV interviewer Harvey Breit, in 1955, "Then I began to write short stories, publicly."

Mixed feelings about having been picked out, but mildly censored, by John Crowe Ransom, were transformed into pure pleasure when Robert Penn Warren selected a story of hers from a pile of student work during a visit to the university in April 1946. Warren had delivered a talk in the Senate Chamber of Old Capitol on his story "Blackberry Winter"; his new novel that year, *All the King's Men*, was awarded the 1947 Pulitzer Prize. Another Southerner, and an editor of her *Understanding Fiction* anthology, "Red" Warren, was one of the more influential writers and critics of the moment. As James B. Hall has recalled, "When R. P. Warren cocked one eye and said, 'By god, I like this paragraph right heahr!'—well, something happened. You were stronger, more daring, more resolved the next time out."

Just as important to Flannery's maturing as a writer was advice she received before the end of the spring semester from Paul Horgan, her instructor in Imaginative Writing, a backup course to the Workshop. Hired in February, "Lt. Col. Paul Horgan," as the student newspaper identified the recently discharged officer, was a novelist and 1946 Guggenheim Fellow. O'Connor later told Betty Hester that "Horgan never even knew I was in the room, I am sure—though once he noted about forty things wrong with a story of mine and I thought him a fine teacher." His advice to the girl he did indeed later remember as "a sort of waif of the art of writing" was to set aside a number of hours daily for writing—same time, same place. That habit became her lifelong regimen, the very soul of her artistic credo. She later shared her discipline with a young writer, in 1957: "I write only about two hours every day because that's all the energy I have, but I don't let anything interfere with those two hours, at the same time and same place . . . Something goes on that makes it easier when it does come well. And the fact is if you don't sit there every day, the day it would come well, you won't be sitting there."

Having flown home for summer break in May because of a national railroad shutdown, in spite of President Truman's call for "strike curbs," O'Connor continued to submit her stories to literary magazines, though with less luck, from Milledgeville. She received two rejection notes over the summer, both from Allen Maxwell, the editor of *Southwest Review*, and both addressed to *Mr.* Flannery O'Connor. Either purposely, or inadvertently, her pen name—especially when stories lacked any stereotypical female romantic touches or domestic details but were full of guns and violence—often caused her to be mistaken for a male writer. In June, Maxwell rejected "Wildcat," a story about an old black man's fear of a prowling beast that was highly imitative of Faulkner's "That Evening Sun." In July, he rejected "The Coat" for moving along "in a rather uncertain manner."

On her return to Currier House in September 1946, for the second year of the two-year program, Flannery was better adjusted to her surroundings and roommates than she had been when she first arrived in Iowa. Now living in a quieter back bedroom on the east side of the ground floor, she was able to experience the plus side of the Iowa Workshop that she later described as "an easier, freer childhood." Her roommate the first semester was Sarah Dawson, a former Wac (Women's Army Corps) from Des Moines, and, the second semester, Martha Bell, a former Wave (Women Accepted for Volunteer Emergency Service) from Mount Pleasant. In the adjoining double bedroom—four women shared a single bathroom—lived Jean Newland, of Belle Plaine, and Barbara Tunnicliff, a business major from Emmetsburg.

Barbara felt that she and Flannery had found in each other "kindred spirits," as they often took walks together around Iowa City, steering clear of any dating or frenzied weekend parties. "They would have house parties once in a while and invite men, but I just didn't feel comfortable with those people," says Barbara Tunnicliff Hamilton. "I don't think either of us went to such things." Together they concocted a pipe dream in which Barbara, the "business woman," would become the "patron" who would contribute to the financial support of the "artist" Flannery. "We both had a sense of humor, almost a sense of the ridiculous," said Barbara Hamilton. "We were both a little offbeat." They exchanged bulky sweatshirts: Flannery's bore a University of Iowa insignia; in return, she gave Barbara one emblazoned with "Georgia" in big, red capital letters.

Yet mostly Barbara just heard, or sensed, Flannery on the other side of the closed door, working. "I didn't bother her when she was doing that," says Barbara Hamilton. The young writer liked to keep things plain: no curtains on the windows; a bare bulb hanging by a long cord from the center of the ceiling. When she was alone, she would pull down the shades and sit at her typewriter with a pile of yellow paper, writing and rewriting. If she wasn't writing, she was reading. As there was no food service in "Grad House," she usually took her breakfast and lunch in the room, often snacking on tins of sardines, or perishables that she kept cool on the windowsill. When Barbara asked Flannery why she worked so obsessively at her writing, she replied that she "had to."

"She was very serious about her mission in life, and had a sort of sense of destiny," says Barbara Hamilton. "She knew she was a great writer. She told me so many times. If I would have heard that from other people, I would have laughed up my sleeve, but not with her. We both agreed that she might never be recognized, but that wasn't the point. The point was to do what she thought she was meant to do." Another woman in the Workshop, Ruth Sullivan, already looked up to Flannery as a writer, and treated her as an authority. "With the door open between our rooms, I often heard bits of their conversations," says Hamilton, of Sullivan soliciting Flannery's opinions. "I remember Ruth once saying she thought maybe she'd better give up trying to write, get married, and have a 'pack of kids.' Flannery seemed always glad to try to help with advice."

In the fall of 1946, the Workshop moved into a sheet-metal Quonset hut on the banks of the Iowa River north of the Iowa Memorial Union; its next move, soon afterward, was to four corrugated-iron barracks. Quickly assembled to accommodate the influx of GI Bill students, in a style dubbed "World War II Ghastly" by knowing vets, these rows of official metal buildings constituted a fitting stage set for much of the fiction being written. "When more than half the class are returned servicemen, and when a good proportion of the fiction being written concerns war experiences, one would naturally expect veterans to disagree on the psychological reactions of story heroes," the *Cedar Rapids Gazette* reported of the Workshop, now numbering thirty-five students. "Men who have served in the navy question the motives of the air corps story heroes; infantry men do the same about the navy."

While not writing about the war, Flannery did try her hand at a topical subject for a next story, "The Barber." In November, a married couple had opened University Barber Shop on East Market Street to accommodate black students unable to get haircuts at "Jim Crow barbers" in town or on the campus. The State University of Iowa president, Virgil M. Hancher, refused to take a position on this divisive issue. For weeks, the Workshop had been abuzz with the topic as its only black member, Herb Nipson, who later became an editor of *Ebony* magazine, needed to travel twenty-one miles to Cedar Rapids to get a haircut. At about this time, Nipson was present at Flannery's reading of a story of hers involving relations between blacks and whites. Afterward a student complimented her dignified, respectful portrayal of a black servant. Nipson has recalled that "Flannery's answer went something like this, 'No. That's just the way he was.'"

In "The Barber," she reset the racial tension to Joe's Barber Shop in Dilton, a fictional college town in the rural South. The story turns on three visits made by Rayber, a liberal college professor, when he argues with its patrons, all supporters of Hawkson, a populist and racist conservative candidate. With little personal knowledge of men's barbershops, she pulled off a convincing evocation of hot lather, tinted windows, and good old boys spitting tobacco. But from its opening line, "It is trying on liberals in Dilton," Rayber was more a brunt of jokes than heroic, lending credence to a suspicion among some in the Workshop that she displayed too much of the "Southern attitude." James B. Hall reports, "She once said to my wife, also a Southerner, 'Momma and me got a nigger that drives us around.' My wife was privately critical of that order of talk."

Yet Flannery's personal attitudes about race were actually quite progressive during her years in Iowa. "I see I should ride the bus more often," she wrote to Betty Hester, in 1957. "I used to when I went to school in Iowa, as I rode the train from Atl. and the bus from M'ville, but no more. Once I heard the driver say to the rear occupants, 'All right, all you stovepipe blonds, git on back there.' At which moment I became an integrationist." Having become friendly for a while with a black woman graduate student, she bucked warnings from her mother that interracial friendships were dangerous, refusing to be swayed by such issues. She joked of "Verge" Hancher, complicit in Southern-style segregation on campus, as being president of the "Iowa Barber School."

Another story she wrote that year was equally a departure. While she had created a morning discipline of daily mass, followed by hours of writing, she had yet to put the two activities together. She had not treated the religious faith that was sustaining her in a story, even a darkly comic one. Her first attempt was "The Turkey," which used as its central symbol the bird she had once drawn in a preschool cartoon. In the story, a little boy, Ruller, "captured" a wild turkey, already shot dead in a ditch, interpreting the prize as a sign of favor from God. The juvenile preacher in training fancies himself, in one draft, "like Billy Graham." Imagining himself into the 1938 film *Boys Town*, "He thought of Bing Crosby and Spencer Tracy. He might have found a place for boys to stay who were going bad." But when his bird is swiped by just such bad boys, his faith becomes mixed with terror: "He was certain that Something Awful was tearing behind him."

As important to the young writer as assiduously imitating the masters were her reading courses. She took Seminar in Literary Criticism, taught by Austin Warren, another rising star among the New Critics, at work at the time with Iowa Professor René Wellek on their landmark *Theory of Literature*. For her supplementary texts in the class of this cultivated, Jamesian gentleman, with a national reputation as an organist, she chose Joyce's *Dubliners* and Brooks and Warren's *Understanding Fiction*. During the class segment on Joyce, Warren treated her as the resident expert in Roman Catholicism, asking, "Now, Miss O'Connor, what are we talking about here?" She took, as well, a two-semester course, Philosophy in Literature; Aesthetics in the Philosophy Department; and Select Contemporary Authors, concentrating on modern European novelists.

By far her most significant literature class was a two-semester independent study, Reading for Final Exam, directed by Engle. "I didn't really start to read until I went to Graduate School and then I began to read and write at the same time," she rattled off her regimen to a friend.

> *Then I began to read everything at once, so much so that I didn't have time I suppose to be influenced by any one writer. I read all the Catholic novelists, Mauriac, Bernanos, Bloy, Green, Waugh; I read all the nuts like Djuna Barnes and Dorothy Richardson and Va. Woolfe (unfair to the dear lady of course). I read the best Southern writers like Faulkner and the Tates, K. A. Porter, Eudora Welty and Peter Taylor; read the Russians, not Tolstoy so much but Dostoyevsky, Turgenev, Chekhov and Gogol. I became a great admirer of Conrad and have read almost all his fiction.*

Around Christmas 1946, Flannery started work on a new story, "The Train." She began with the conscious intent to build a novel from its tale of Hazel Wickers, a nineteen-year-old, homesick, country rube returning South after the war. In choosing a first name as unisexual as her own, she relied on a custom she happily noticed among rural families who occasionally gave their sons feminine names—June, for instance. Her readings in Joyce and Faulkner were echoed in neologisms like "greyflying" to describe the train whizzing by. Yet what truly caught her imagination was a train ride home for the holidays. As she later explained the genesis of the story, "It started when I was on a train coming from Chicago. There was a Tennessee boy on it in uniform who was much taken up worrying the porter about how the berths were made up; the porter was so regal he just barely tolerated the boy."

On the first leg of that holiday trip, Flannery made her way across downtown Chicago from LaSalle Street Station to Dearborn Station, "a journey that never impressed me as beautiful." She then caught the Dixie Limited, to travel from Illinois through Tennessee to Georgia. A discarded draft gives a glimpse, through Hazel's eyes, of "the dilapidated [Dearborn] station, where the southern trains came in. There was a strange feeling in it for him, of awayness and homeness mixed . . . It was a sooted red brick with turrets and inside it was gray and smoked and there were spittoons parked at the end of every third bench." O'Connor later delighted in telling a friend of one of her own encounters at the terminus, "I sat down next to a colored woman in the waiting room at the Dearborn Street station in Chicago once. She was eating grapes and asked me to have some but I declined. She was very talkative and kept talking and eating grapes. Finally she asked me where I was from and I said, 'Georgia,' and she spit a mouthful of grape seeds out on the floor and said, 'My God,' and got up and left."

Flickering through various drafts of "The Train," marked "Workshop," is the presence of a more military Haze, recently demobilized, among army buddies en route, like Flannery, from Chicago to Chattanooga. In one version, he is the life of the party, buying them all beers in the club car and passing out cigarettes. While keeping quiet in class, Flannery had evidently been listening closely to the war stories of classmates, like Jim Ericcson, at work on a novel about a veteran in a hospital, suffering, he told the *Cedar Rapids Gazette*, from "the Oedipus complex." She borrowed from these war-torn heroes for her own more comic antihero. And although Iowa City never left many traces in her fiction, the minute she hit Dearborn

Station, where Hazel felt "a thump of recognition" at hearing "flat and twangish" country voices, her imagination clicked on.

When she returned to Iowa City in January 1947, Flannery set to work finishing "The Train," the last of the six stories in her thesis collection, the writing requirement for an MFA degree. She also began adapting the story as the first chapter of her novel in progress. The novel was inspired not simply by themes of "awayness" and "homeness," but also by Paul Engle's announcement in November of an award from Rinehart Publishers of a $750 advance for a novel, to be awarded to a Workshop student in May, with an option, upon acceptance, of another $750. Engle had already sent two of her stories to his friend John Selby, the Rinehart editor in charge of the prize. Flush from the success of their recent best-selling novels, *The Lost Weekend* by Charles R. Jackson, and *The Hucksters* by Frederic Wakeman, the publishers hoped to sign up hot new talent.

For help with writing the required outline and four chapters, or twelve thousand words, she turned to Andrew Lytle, brought in by Engle as a visiting lecturer and instructor in February and put up in Quonset hut no. 244. Tall and wiry, Lytle, in his midforties, was a card-carrying Southerner and gentleman farmer. As an undergraduate at Vanderbilt University in Nashville, he had been one of the original members of the Agrarians, a literary movement nostalgic for Old South rural, aristocratic values. Before leaving college to go off to Yale Drama School and a stint as a Broadway actor, he was friendly with the founding Fugitive poets, including Allen Tate, Donald Davidson, and Robert Penn Warren. In "The Hind Tit," the essay he contributed to the 1930 Agrarian manifesto, *I'll Take My Stand*, he wrote of Tennessee yeomen farmers, much like Hazel, displaced from the land by the "pizen snake" of industrialism.

Lytle first encountered Flannery while sitting in on a Workshop class, where he was asked to read her student story aloud: "I was told later that it was understood that I would know how to pronounce in good country idiom the word chitling which appeared in the story. At once it was obvious that the author of the story was herself not only

Southern but exceptionally gifted." Flannery responded to Lytle as a protective big brother and consummate prose stylist, known to "make a federal case out of a comma." It fell to Lytle to help her through a scene involving Hazel and a prostitute that wound up in the novel's second chapter: "She would put a man in bed with a woman, and I would say, 'Now, Flannery, it's not done quite that way,' and we talked a little bit about it, but she couldn't face up to it, so she put a hat on his head and made a comic figure of him." He advised her to "sink the theme" and "clobber" her reader more subtly.

Their master-apprentice relationship irritated those students baffled by the growing recognition of the young lady meanly described by one as having "a bale of cotton in her mouth." Aware of the rumblings, Lytle said, "She was a lovely girl, but scared the boys to death with her irony." Lytle did not help matters by talking widely of her talent. "Why, she can just walk by a poolroom and know exactly what's happening by the smell," he told James B. Hall, the "second best" writer in class. As the Brooklyn native Eugene Brown explains, "People who were favored in the Writers' Workshop at that time were Southern writers." This suspicion of Southern loyalty was only confirmed with the campus visit during the week of April 21 of the Fugitive poet and *Sewanee Review* editor Allen Tate. In his class "critique," Tate likewise paid special attention to Lytle's protégée.

Flannery was busily filling out applications and gathering together her finished manuscripts by early May 1947. First she applied for several college teaching positions, just in case. "It comes to us all," she moaned of the dreaded profession. She then enlisted Barbara Tunnicliff to type her thesis project, *The Geranium: A Collection of Short Stories.* "She paid me for doing it and watched over me as I did," recalled her former suitemate. O'Connor dedicated the work, for his extraordinary support, "To Paul Engle, whose interest and criticism have made these stories better than they would otherwise have been." Norma Hodges remembers helping Flannery and a mutual friend, Carol Nutter, carry stacks of its pages from the print shop. According to Hodges, continuously feeling shunned by her, when they arrived at the door of Nutter's second-floor apartment, Flannery coldly discouraged her from entering, wishing to be alone with her friend Carol: "Her magnified eyes swam up punctuating an unspoken, 'Don't you dare come in!'"

In the synopsis required for her Rinehart application, O'Connor hinted that a starting point, if not blueprint, for Haze's quest might be found in T. S. Eliot's shattered epic of modern life, *The Waste Land*, a poem revered by her New Critic writer-instructors: "His search for a physical home mirrors his search for a spiritual one, and although he finds neither, it is the latter search which saves him from becoming a member of the Wasteland and makes him worth 75,000 words."

Partly the reference was parody, a use of a buzzword. But unlike her joke on Proust in high school, she was reading Eliot's poems and essays very closely and sympathetically. As a poet at once modern and devout, having converted to Anglo-Catholicism a decade after writing his poem of "fragments I have shored against my ruins," Eliot was a figure of fascination to O'Connor. Traces of this deep interest dot her Iowa pages: a "dead geranium" is a central image of his poem "Rhapsody on a Windy Night"; the fortune-teller Madame Sosostris of *The Waste Land* shows up in a draft of her novel as Madame Sosistra; her mummy's colloquial museum label, "once as tall as you or me," is lifted from Eliot's line about Phlebas the Phoenician, "once as handsome and tall as you."

All of this hard work finally paid off during the fourth week in May, when she received official word that she was the winner of the Rinehart-Iowa Award, and that Engle had pulled strings to secure her a teaching assistantship for the following year. In an interview accompanying her photograph and front-page story in the *Daily Iowan*, she insisted that her novel about a man searching for a spiritual home was not a "typed" novel: "Any author who follows a hard and fast outline allows himself to become a slave to the typewriter." To celebrate, on May 29 she traveled by car to Cedar Rapids with her roommate, Martha Bell, and housemother, Sarah Dawson. "We had dinner there," Bell recorded in her diary, "did some window-shopping and then went to see *The Egg and I.*" The plot of the light romantic comedy they chose concerned a society girl (Claudette Colbert) who is persuaded by her new husband (Fred MacMurray) to start a chicken farm.

Also celebrating the end of the semester, Paul Engle and his wife, Mary, threw a picnic at Stone City, their Victorian summer house, previously belonging to Grant Wood, next to a limestone quarry. Charles Embree, a Missouri writer whose first Workshop story, "Concerning the Mop," about jazz, had just been published in *Esquire*, drove Flannery to the party in his 1936 Ford coupe. Because of his Southern accent, Flannery often asked him to read her stories in class. "She was a loner," says Embree. "Yet everybody respected her talent. It was apparent." In one photograph of a dozen guests taken that day at the quarry, Flannery stands off to the side, in a heavy dark skirt and checked jacket. In a crowded group portrait in the living room, she is hidden behind the woman next to her, with only her knee showing. "It was wholly typical of Flannery that the part of her visible is the right knee," wrote Engle. "There is a spirit about that knee."

Springtime parties, no matter what the excuse, were the norm in Iowa City because of the demands of the extreme winters; the guests at Stone City that afternoon were mostly in high spirits simply from the mild break in the weather. "In spring, it was as though we had come through," wrote James B. Hall. "The Iowa countryside was one long, low lyric of fields growing." For the trip back, Andrew Lytle offered rides to both James Hall and Flannery, who tucked herself silently into the backseat, her extreme quietness making her more a potent presence. Hall recalls that "Andrew was talking about Flannery's recent distinction, her Rinehart Award. He was driving, but looked closely at me, also in the front seat. I thought he was rubbing it in, and also seeing how I was taking the news."

In the days immediately following, Flannery returned to Milledgeville for the summer, where she joined the Cline family, still mourning the sudden death of Uncle Bernard at the end of January.

Her relatives were trying to deal with the practicalities of his will, including his bequest of Sorrel Farm to Regina and Louis. On a bus trip to Atlanta in the fall of 1946, Flannery had chanced to sit next to a descendant of the Hawkins family, the original owners, who informed her that the farm, in the nineteenth century, had been called Andalusia, after a province of southern Spain. She wrote her mother, pushing for reinstating its fanciful name, and her uncle Bernard had been willing. So Andalusia it now was. "I was in Milledgeville in the summer of 1947 with my mother," says Frances Florencourt. "I remember Flannery was very happy, upbeat, smiling." The hopeful twenty-two-year-old was in a good humor that season.

A postgraduate student on a fellowship, Flannery made independent living arrangements when she returned to Iowa City in September for her final year. As a teaching assistant, she was given an office in the Old Dental Building next to University Hall, reserved for junior members of the English faculty. After looking at a number of boardinghouses, she settled on renting a single room in a big, gray, wood-frame house at 115 East Bloomington Street, owned by a Mrs. Guzeman. Like the boardinghouse of Haze Motes in *Wise Blood*, her new address was "clapboard . . . in a block of them, all alike." And like Haze's Mrs. Flood, her own "Mrs." landlady, whom she surmised "was most a hundred then," could be penurious. As she later groused, "Mrs. Guzeman was not very fond of me because I stayed at home and required heat to be on—at least ON. It was never UP that I remember. When it was on you could smell it and I got to where I warmed up a little every time I smelled it."

On the opening day of the Workshop, she made friends with Jean Williams, a new student-writer from Indianapolis, who sat down in the seat beside her. "Flannery was sitting alone in the front row, over against the wall," wrote Jean Williams Wylder. "She was wearing what I was soon to think of as her 'uniform' for the year: plain gray skirt and neatly ironed silkish blouse, nylon stockings and penny brown loafers. Her only makeup was a trace of lipstick . . . there was something of the convent about Flannery that day—a certain intentness in the slight girlish figure which set her apart from the rest of us. She seemed out of place in that room composed mostly of veterans returned from World War II. Flannery was only twenty-two years old then, but . . . could easily have passed for seventeen or eighteen."

Jean Williams saw her only a few times that fall, outside of the Monday afternoon Workshop sessions. As Mrs. Guzeman didn't serve Sunday dinner, Flannery occasionally took her noon meal at the Mad Hatter Tea Room, over Bremer's Clothing Store, on Washington Street, where Williams worked as a "salad girl." They once bumped into each other as she was exiting Woolworth's Five-and-Ten-Cent Store with a single cake of Palmolive soap. "I doubt if Flannery ever bought two of anything at one time," she recalled. When Williams visited O'Connor's room at Mrs. Guzeman's, she was struck by the "monastic simplicity" of its "neatly made bed, the typewriter waiting on a desk. There was nothing extraneous in that room except a box of vanilla wafers beside the typewriter. She nibbled on cookies while she wrote, she said, because she didn't smoke."

A more involved friendship began at the same time with Robie Macauley. On leave for the year, Engle put Andrew Lytle in charge of the Workshop and brought in Macauley as both a student and instructor, teaching a course in Russian literature. "He was a brilliant young professor," says Bernie Halperin, a Workshop writer who took his course. "He was a thin, nice-looking fellow, with a tremendous knowledge of those massive Russian novels." At the age of twenty-eight, the Michigan native had earned a BA at Kenyon College, where he studied under John Crowe Ransom; served during the war in the Army Counterintelligence Corps; taught at Bard College; and worked as an editor at Henry Holt and Company. Upon first hearing O'Connor read from her novel in progress, he was immediately impressed by the work as "entirely original, strange."

"I used to date Flannery and I remember sitting with her long hours on the porch swing of her boardinghouse . . . discussing a number of deep matters or reading the new chapters of *Wise Blood*, which she was writing at the time," Macauley later recounted. "As for the deep matters, I remember that Flanders Dunbar had become intellectually fashionable that year and we'd both read her, and so we spent a lot of time discussing psychosomatic medicine." The Dunbar book was *Mind and Body*, its author also a medievalist with an interest in Dante, a favorite of the two new friends. Macauley also occasionally escorted Flannery, with Workshop instructor Paul Griffith and his girlfriend, to Sunday lunch in Amana, the historic German Pietist community, twenty miles from Iowa City: "We ate in a big barnlike dining hall with everybody at long tables. Flannery liked that."

During the fall, Macauley introduced Flannery to his friends Walter Sullivan, a Workshop writer from Tennessee, and his wife, Jane. "Robie took care of Flannery . . . he had a gift of making her relax," Sullivan had observed of their easygoing relationship. When Macauley first brought her by a small party at their home, promising, "There's a little Georgia girl here you've got to meet," she found an audience highly receptive to spun tales of her childhood, especially her centerpiece story of the Pathe News arriving to film her backward-walking chicken. "Flannery would get strung out and start telling stories about the South," said Jane Sullivan of her many visits. "Funny stories, and it was hysterical, but this required a small group for conversation; it wasn't party stuff."

Regarding his friendship with Flannery, Macauley used the term "date" a couple of times with interviewers. Yet whatever dating occurred was of the lightest sort. As he explained when pressed, "Flannery and I had no 'romantic' relationship. I was engaged to Anne Draper (who was in New York) and Flannery was well aware of it . . . We did spend a lot of time talking and reading manuscripts." Her bond with the tall, soft-spoken intellectual, not a "party man," was more as a "soul mate." Like the soldier John Sullivan, he was a good-looking, somewhat unavailable, slightly older guy who protected and encouraged her. And she brought a similar excitement to their friendship. Once Jean Williams saw Flannery on her way to the library to check out Gogol's *Dead Souls*, which Macauley told her was a must-read for every writer. "So I reckon I better do it," Flannery said.

The first week in October a dorm mate of Macauley's from Kenyon, Robert Lowell, arrived to give a poetry reading in the Old Capitol and to critique Workshop poems. A Boston-born disciple of the Fugitives, Lowell had camped out during the summer of 1937 in the backyard of Allen Tate and his wife, Caroline Gordon, in Tennessee, to learn at the feet of the Vanderbilt masters; he then broke with family tradition by leaving Harvard to study, like Macauley, as one of "Ransom's boys," at Kenyon. Later describing Iowa City as "tame and friendly," the thirty-year-old poet, in 1947, was treated as a wild celebrity. Chain-smoking, curly-haired, and unruly, he cut a poetic figure. "He was so sensitive, he trembled as he read to us," recalls James B. Hall. Flannery was quite impressed by Lowell, at the reading and at a dinner, where he held forth one night during his four-day visit.

A visitor altogether different from Robert Lowell arrived later in the month for a weekend stay—Mary Virginia Harrison, her attractive "best friend" from high school. Mary Virginia stayed at a hotel, and one night the girlfriends shared a double bed at Mrs. Guzeman's. Flannery had written that she could meet her train at any hour, as her own life was "simple, austere." As for clothing, she advised, "The well dressed Iowa Citian is usually seen in a sweat shirt, trousers or skirt (as the sex may dictate), heavy coat and limp cigaret." A Georgia State College for Women classmate they both knew was Faye Hancock, married to the Workshop writer Hank Messick, and living in Victory Park, a student trailer park for veterans. Messick later recalled that on her visits Flannery preferred bottled Blue Ridge springwater. "When it was gone," he wrote, "she returned to mixed drinks, claiming a lot of Scotch was necessary to make the water drinkable."

For her third holiday trip home to Milledgeville that December, Flannery was accompanied as far as La Salle Street Station in Chicago by Jean Williams. The train ride in high-backed swivel chairs in the parlor car was their longest time spent together. Flannery convinced the porter it would be "right nice" if he would "allow" her friend into the first-class section, too. She was putting the final touches that month on "The Train," which would be published in April in the *Sewanee Review*, the prestigious quarterly from Tennessee's University of the South, edited by both Lytle and Tate. "They know exactly what they're doing all the time," she said, eyeing the porter. "No dilly-dallying at all." She then took out a snapshot of the Cline Mansion from her purse to show. "Flannery was glad to be going home that Christmas," wrote Jean Williams Wylder. "She looked very pretty, more like a college girl . . . almost tall in a blue plaid suit and tan polo jacket."

When they both returned to Iowa City, Jean accompanied Flannery on a walk that doubled as a fact-finding mission. At work on a chapter about Haze's lone friend, Enoch Emery, at City Forest Park Zoo, Flannery suggested they visit the local City Park Zoo, a half-mile walk along the Iowa River. Here she got her inspiration for Enoch's fixation on a cage of "two black bears . . . sitting and facing each other like two matrons having tea," which she worked into her story "The Heart of the Park." According to her friend, on this bleak Sunday afternoon in February, a "completely absorbed and interested" Flannery stared at "the two sad and mangy bears, the raccoons, and the special foreign chickens they had." O'Connor later remembered "two indifferent bears . . . and a sign over them that said: 'These lions donated by the Iowa City Elks Club.'"

If her "barbarous Georgia accent," as she joked of it, had been a liability two years earlier, during the spring of 1948 readings by Flannery were much sought after. One circle where she felt comfortable sharing her work gathered on Sunday evenings at Austin Warren's elegant home. The in-group included Robie Macauley; Andrew Lytle; Warren Miller, reading from a Kafkaesque novel in progress; and Clyde McLeod, one of only three women in the Workshop that year, who sang a ballad with a "Hootie, Hootie" refrain. "Flannery's novel is sure going to be very beautiful," Paul Griffith reported in mid-February to Engle, still on leave; "her chapter at AW's was polished and colored to perfection." Hansford Martin, an instructor in the Workshop, annoyed by her endless revisions, complained to Engle that "Flannery, in spite of all that Paul and I say, is still rewriting her first chapter."

Another such informal Midwestern salon took place in the rented rooms of the writer John Gruen and the painter Jane Wilson, then both MFA students at Iowa. "We would invite her to our house because we had little gatherings, and ask her to read," says Gruen. "She would sit quietly at first until she was asked to read. 'Okay, Flannery, did you bring your story?' 'Yeeees.' 'Are you going to read it?' 'Yeeees.' I believe that she read the first chapters of her novel in an accent that was even fiercer than the way she regularly spoke. She took on all the characters. She would read in this kind of very heavy singsong but not really singing. It was a performance. It became totally hypnotic. So that all of us sitting there, young people in their teens and twenties, were totally struck."

In early drafts of her novel, Hazel had a sister, Ruby Hill, a "modern" type who lives in a boardinghouse and, upon discovering she is pregnant, wishes to have an abortion. The bit Jane Wilson recalls Flannery reading was a version of this subplot, later spun off by the "demon rewriter," as Robie Macauley dubbed his friend, into "Woman on the Stairs," published the next summer in *Tomorrow*, a small literary magazine, and eventually revised and published as "A Stroke of Good Fortune." "She read the story in this rhythm of a woman climbing a stair," remembers Wilson. "It was so persuasive. It was a monologue of silly miseries and dismay. 'Oh this waistband is so uncomfortable on me. Oh, God!' Then in the end when she gets to the top of the stairs her worst fears have burst through. It's not weight gain. She's pregnant . . . The writing was scary. But she emanated warmth while she was reading it . . . affection, in a way."

Over the course of the spring, Flannery was given guidance in planning her future. As Norma Hodges suggests, "She had this air of dependence about her, as if she needed someone to take care of her." Engle arranged a teaching fellowship for the following year. Griffith suggested applying for a summer residency at the Yaddo artists' colony in Saratoga Springs, New York. He then helped her gather a strong list of recommendations. Austin Warren endorsed her as "a personally shy but kind and charming young Southern writer." Andrew Lytle wrote that she had "as much promise as anyone I have seen of her generation." Engle praised her as "one of the best young writers in the country." Her application was successful, and Hansford Martin reported to Engle in April, "Flannery seems happiest of all, blossoming like a rose, packing for Yaddo."

She was happy enough even to overcome her reluctance to read aloud in the Workshop. In the class run that spring by Lytle, Flannery had rarely spoken up. Once, when her mentor asked her to comment on a student's story, she paused a beat, then in a deadpan voice, she replied laconically, "I'd say the description of that crocodile in there was real good." For her memorable late-April performance, she chose to read the vignette of the woman on the stairs, which she introduced as the second chapter of her novel. Her "flat, nasal drawl" reminded the Workshop writer Gene Brzenk of the comic screen actress Zasu Pitts, known for her switchboard operator voice. "She never looked up," he recalled, "and acknowledged her audience only when the laughter drowned out her voice. When she finished reading, we all applauded and the meeting broke up in high good humor."

At the close of the afternoon, Flannery quickly disappeared through the door to return to her room, while the other students regrouped for beers at the Brown Derby, a hangout on Dubuque Street. But Jean Williams turned to Clyde McLeod, unsatisfied. "For once there was not going to be any critical dissecting," Jean Williams Wylder had written. "That we had said nothing about Flannery's story was a tribute to her genius. But, the other girl writer and I wanted there to be something more—some more tangible token of our admiration. We went around Iowa City on that late spring afternoon, walking into people's yards as if they were public domain, to gather arms full of flowering branches—taking only the most beautiful— and we carried them up to Flannery."

Open City Index (Issues 1–26)

Abreu, Jean Claude and Jorge Jauregui, trans., "The First Visit to the Louvre: Fragments of an Improbable Dialogue" (story) by Rafael Fernández de Villa-Urrutia. *Open City* 16 (2002–2003): 177-181.

Acconci, Vito. Three poems. *Open City* 5 (1997): 99–102.

Adams, Bill. "Interior, Exterior, Portrait, Still-Life, Landscape" (drawings). *Open City* 19 (2004): 73–83.

Alcalá, Rosa, trans., "The Brilliance of Orifices," "Mother of Pearl," "The Anatomy of Paper" (poems) by Cecilia Vicuña. *Open City* 14 (2001–2002): 151–154.

Alcalay, Ammiel, trans., "Hotel," "Precautionary Manifesto" (poems) by Semezdin Mehmedinovic. *Open City* 17 (2003): 141-142.

Alcalay, Henry. "Learn to Drive Trucks Big Money" (story). *Open City* 26 (2008–2009): 81–100.

Ali, Mohammed Naseehu. "The Long Ride Back Home" (story). *Open City* 26 (2008–2009): 1–14.

Allen, Roberta. "Surreal" (story). *Open City* 9 (1999): 53–54.

Altmann, Howard. "Stones," "Gymnast in the Dark," "Island," "Sunday Monday" (poems). *Open City* 25: 177–182.

Alvaraz, A. Two Untitled Poems. *Open City* 3 (1995): 72–74.

Ames, Greg. "Physical Discipline" (story). *Open City* 17 (2003): 209–216.

Ames, Jonathan. "Writer for Hire: A Spencer Johns Story" (story). *Open City* 9 (1999): 55-68.

Ames, Jonathan. "I Was in Flowers" (story). *Open City* 25 (2008): 39–44

Anderson, Jack. "Elsewhere," "Believing in Ghosts" (poems). *Open City* 19 (2004): 51–53.

Anderson, Lucy. "Another Fish Poem" (poem). *Open City* 4 (1996): 195–196.

Andoe, Joe. "This Would Be the Day All My Dreams Come True," "Fence," "Seeing Red," "Eighteen-Year-Old Stucco Laborer and White Crosses" (poems). *Open City* 16 (2002–2003): 59–62.

Anderson, Lucy. "Winter Solstice," "Reentry," "What If, Then Nothing" (poems). *Open City* 9 (1999): 141–144.

Antoniadis, Tony. "Rescue 907!" (story). *Open City* 20 (2005): 181–193.

Arnold, Craig. "SSSSSSHHHHHH," "There is a circle drawn around you," "Your friend's arriving on the bus" (poems). *Open City* 16 (2002–2003): 97–105.

Badanes, Jerome. "Change Or Die" (unfinished novel). *Open City* 5 (1997): 159–233.

Badanes, Jerome. "The Man in the Twelve Thousand Rooms" (essay). *Open City* 23 (2007): 1–3.

Badanes, Jerome. "Guinea Golden," "From Day to Day," "Late Night Footsteps on the Staircase" (poems). *Open City* 23 (2007): 5–10.

Bakowski, Peter. "The Width of the World," "We Are So Rarely Out of the Line of Fire" (poems). *Open City* 11 (2000): 95–100.

Balkenhol, Stephan. Drawings. *Open City* 5 (1997): 38–42.

Bar-Nadav, Hadara. "Talking to Strangers" (story). *Open City* 23 (2007): 11–23.

Bar-Nadav, Hadara. "Bricolage and Blood," "I Used to Be Snow White," "To Halve and to Hole" (poems). *Open City* 23 (2007): 25–29.

Bartók-Baratta, Edward. "Walker" (poem). *Open City* 18 (2003–2004): 175.

Battle, Jay. "People Like This Hate People Like You" (drawings). *Open City* 24 (2007–2008): 119–124.

Baum, Erica. "The Following Information" (photographs). *Open City* 13 (2001): 87–94.

Baumbach, Jonathan. "Lost Car" (story). *Open City* 22 (2006): 27–35.

Baumbach, Jonathan. "Travels with Wizard" (story) *Open City* 24 (2007–2008): 125–136.

Baumbach, Nico. "Guilty Pleasure" (story). *Open City* 14 (2001–2002): 39–58.

Beal, Daphne. "Eternal Bliss" (story). *Open City* 12 (2001): 171–190.

Beatty, Paul. "All Aboard" (poem). *Open City* 3 (1995): 245–247.

Becker, Priscilla. "Blue Statuary," "Instrumental" (poems). *Open City* 18 (2003–2004): 151–152.

Becker, Priscilla. "Recurrence of Childhood Paralysis," "Blue Statuary" (poems). *Open City* 19 (2004): 33–34.

Becker, Priscilla. "Typochondria" (essay). *Open City* 22 (2006): 9–12.

Becker, Priscilla. "Math Poem," "Midwestern," "afters," "Desert," "Hatred of Men with Blonde Eyebrows" (poems). *Open City* 26 (2008–2009): 15–20.

Beckman, Joshua and Tomaz Salamun, trans., "VI," "VII" (poems) by Tomaz Salamun. *Open City* 15 (2002): 155–157.

Beckman, Joshua and Matthew Rohrer. "Still Life with Woodpecker," "The Book of Houseplants" (poems). *Open City* 19 (2004): 177–178.

Belcourt, Louise. "Snake, World Drawings" (drawings). *Open City* 14 (2001–2002): 59–67.

Bellamy, Dodie. "From *Cunt-Ups*" (poems). *Open City* 14 (2001–2002): 155–157.

Beller, Thomas. "Vas *Is* Dat?" (story). *Open City* 10 (2000): 51–88.

Bellows, Nathaniel. "At the House on the Lake," "A Certain Dirge," "An Attempt" (poems). *Open City* 16 (2002–2003): 69–73.

Dannatt, Adrian. Introduction to "The House Where I Was Born." *Open City* 7 (1999): 112–115.

Dannatt, Adrian. "Days of Or" (story). *Open City* 8 (1999): 87–96.

Dannatt, Adrian. "Central Park Wet" (story). *Open City* 10 (2000): 103–114.

Dannatt, Trevor. "Night Thoughts (I)," "Night Thoughts (II)" (poems). *Open City* 19 (2004): 133–134.

Daum, Meghan. "Inside the Tube" (essay). *Open City* 12 (2001): 287–304.

David, Stuart. "A Peacock's Wings" (story). *Open City* 13 (2001): 133–138.

Davies, Howell. "The House Where I Was Born" (story). *Open City* 7 (1999): 116–119.

Deller, Jeremy. "The English Civil War (Part II)" (photographs). *Open City* 9 (1999): 159–166.

Delvoye, Wim. Drawings, text. *Open City* 2 (1993): 39–42.

DeMarinis, Rick. "The Life and Times of a Forty-Nine Pound Man" (story). *Open City* 17 (2003): 185–196.

Dermont, Amber. "Number One Tuna" (story). *Open City* 19 (2004): 95–105.

Dezuviria, Sacundo. Photograph. *Open City* 2 (1993): back cover.

Dietrich, Bryan D. "This Island Earth" (poem). *Open City* 16 (2002–2003): 201–202.

Dietrich, Bryan D. "The Thing That Couldn't Die" (poem). *Open City* 21 (2005–2006): 89–90.

Dikeou, Devon. Photographs, drawings, and text. *Open City* 1 (1992): 39–48.

Dikeou, Devon. "Marilyn Monroe Wanted to Be Buried In Pucci" (photographs, drawings, text,). *Open City* 10 (2000): 207–224.

Donnelly, Mary. "Lonely" (poem). *Open City* 12 (2001): 151–152.

Doris, Stacy. "Flight" (play). *Open City* 14 (2001–2002): 147–150.

Dormen, Lesley. "Gladiators" (story). *Open City* 18 (2003–2004): 155–163.

Douglas, Norman. "Male Order" (story). *Open City* 19 (2004): 151–163.

Dowe, Tom. "Legitimation Crisis" (poem). *Open City* 7 (1999): 21.

Doyle, Ben. "And on the First Day" (poem). *Open City* 12 (2001): 203–204.

Duhamel, Denise. "The Frog and the Feather" (story). *Open City* 5 (1997): 115–117.

Dyer, Geoff. "Albert Camus" (story). *Open City* 9 (1999): 23–38.

Grennan, Eamon. "Two Poems" (poems). *Open City* 5 (1997): 137–140.

Eisenegger, Erich. "A Ticket for Kat" (story). *Open City* 16 (2002–2003): 133–141.

Ellison, Lori. "Coffee Drawings" (drawings). *Open City* 13 (2001): 57–66.

Ellison, Lori. Drawing. *Open City* 17 (2003): back cover.

Ellman, Juliana. "Interior, Exterior, Portrait, Still-Life, Landscape" (drawings). *Open City* 19 (2004): 73–83.

Foreman, Richard. "Eddie Goes to Poetry City" (excerpted story, drawings). *Open City* 2 (1993): 63–70.

Fox, Jason. "Models and Monsters" (paintings, drawings). *Open City* 17 (2003): 51–58.

Francis, Juliana. "The Baddest Natashas" (play). *Open City* 13 (2001): 149–172.

Friedman, Bruce Jay. "Lost" (story). *Open City* 16 (2002–2003): 185–190.

Friedman, Stan. "Male Pattern Baldness" (poem). *Open City* 1 (1992): 13–14.

Fuss, Adam. "Untitled" (photograph). *Open City* 6 (1998): front cover.

Gaddis, Anicée. "Fast and Slow" (story). *Open City* 20 (2005): 123–135.

Gaitskill, Mary. "The Crazy Person" (story). *Open City* 1 (1992): 49–61.

Gaitskill, Mary. "The Rubbed-Away Girl" (story). *Open City* 7 (1999): 137–148.

Gaffney, Elizabeth, trans., "Given" (story) by Alissa Walser. *Open City* 8 (1999): 141–149.

Galchen, Rivka. "Wild Berry Blue" (story). *Open City* 25 (2008): 69–84.

de Ganay, Sebastien. "Überfremdung" (paintings). *Open City* 11 (2000): 189–198.

Garrison, Deborah. "An Idle Thought," "Father, R.I.P., Sums Me Up at Twenty-Three," "A Friendship Enters Phase II" (poems). *Open City* 6 (1998): 21–26.

Garrison, Deborah. "Giving Notice" (letter). *Open City* 23 (2007): 79–80.

Garrison, Deborah. "A Short Skirt on Broadway," "Add One," "Both Square and Round," "The Necklace" (poems). *Open City* 23 (2007): 81–88.

Gerety, Meghan. Drawings. *Open City* 10 (2000): 151–158.

Gersh, Amanda. "On Safari" (story). *Open City* 10 (2000): 135–150.

Gifford, William. "Fight" (story). *Open City* 4 (1996): 207–214.

Gilbert, Josh. "Hack Wars" (story). *Open City* 18 (2003–2004): 55–60.

Gillick, Liam. "Signage for a Four Story Building" (art project). *Open City* 8 (1999): 121–125.

Gillison, Samantha. "Petty Cash" (story). *Open City* 4 (1996): 197–206.

Ginsberg, Allen. Photograph and text. *Open City* 3 (1995): 191–194.

Gizzi, Peter. "Take the 5:01 to Dreamland" (poem). *Open City* 17 (2003): 151–152.

Gold, Herbert. "Next In Line" (story). *Open City* 22 (2006): 65–69.

Goldstein, Jesse. "Dance With Me Ish, Like When You Was a Baby" (story). *Open City* 17 (2003): 197–199.

Golliver, Benjamin. "Las Vegas Bypass" (essay). *Open City* 26 (2008–2009): 121–130.

Gonzales, Mark. "To You, My Reader" (story). *Open City* 8 (1999): 153–154.

Gonzalez, Manuel. "The Disappearance of the Sebali Tribe" (story). *Open City* 22 (2006): 49–64.

Hartenbach, Mark. "emotional triage in assorted shapes & colors," "a two-toned oldsmobile going 85 mph," "sodium nitrate" (poems). *Open City* 24 (2007–2008): 69–71.

Harvey, Ellen. "Friends and Their Knickers" (paintings). *Open City* 6 (1998): 133–144.

Harvey, Ellen. "100 Visitors to the Biennial Immortalized" (drawings and text). *Open City* 25 (2008): 51–62.

Harvey, Matthea. "Sergio Valente, Sergio Valente, How You Look Tells the World How You Feel," "To Zanzibar By Motorcar" (poems). *Open City* 18 (2003–2004): 97–98.

Haug, James. "Everything's Jake" (poem). *Open City* 18 (2003–2004): 193.

Hauser, Thomas. "Schmetterlinge und Butterblumen" (drawings). *Open City* 12 (2001): 131–136.

Hayashi, Toru. "Equivocal Landscape" (drawings). *Open City* 12 (2001): 43–48.

Hayes, Michael. "Police Blotter." *Open City* 8 (1999): 107–110.

Healey, Steve. "The Asshole of the Immanent," "Tilt" (poems). *Open City* 15 (2002): 77–80.

Healy, Tom. "What the Right Hand Knows" (poem). *Open City* 17 (2003): 113–114.

Heeman, Christoph. "Pencil Drawings" (drawings). *Open City* 17 (2003): 91–98.

Hendriks, Martijn. "Swerve" (story). *Open City* 21 (2005–2006): 31–34.

Henry, Brian. "I Lost My Tooth on the Way to Plymouth (Rock)," "Intro to Lit" (poems). *Open City* 18 (2003–2004): 139–140.

Henry, Max and Sam Samore. "Hobo Deluxe, A Cinema of Poetry" (photographs and text). *Open City* 12 (2001): 257–270.

Henry, Peter. "Thrift" (poem). *Open City* 7 (1999): 136.

Hedegaard, Erik. "The La-Z-Boy Position" (story). *Open City* 4 (1996): 117–121.

Heyd, Suzanne. "Mouth Door I," "Mouth Door II" (poems). *Open City* 20 (2005): 175–179.

Higgs, Matthew. "Three Parts" and "Photograph of a Book (I Married an Artist)" (photographs). *Open City* 16 (2002–2003): 203–210; front and back covers.

Hill, Amy. "Psycho-narratives" (paintings). *Open City* 14 (2001–2002): 89–95.

Hillesland, Ann. "Ultimate Catch" (story). *Open City* 22 (2006): 37–47.

Hocking, Justin. "Dragon" (story). *Open City* 18 (2003–2004): 123–138.

Hoffman, Cynthia Marie. "Dear Commercial Street," (poem). *Open City* 17 (2003): 125–127.

Hofstede, Hilarius. "The Marquis Von Water" (text art project). *Open City* 3 (1995): 135–144.

Hogan, John Brinton. "Vacation" (photographs). *Open City* 20 (2005): 113–120.

Katchadourian, Nina. "Selections from *The Sorted Books Project*" (photographs). *Open City* 16 (2002–2003): 143–153.

Kazanas, Luisa. "Drawings" (drawings). *Open City* 13 (2001): 139–146.

Kean, Steve. Paintings. *Open City* 4 (1996): 129–133.

Keegan, Claire. "Surrender" (story). *Open City* 24 (2007–2008): 73–84.

Kenealy, Ryan. "Yellow and Maroon" (story). *Open City* 7 (1999): 60–70.

Kenealy, Ryan. "Resuscitation of the Shih Tzu" (story). *Open City* 16 (2002–2003): 89–96.

Kenealy, Ryan. "God's New Math" (story). *Open City* 20 (2005): 209–216.

Kennedy, Hunter. "Nice Cool Beds" (story). *Open City* 6 (1998): 162–174.

Kennedy, Hunter. "When Is It That You Feel Good?" (poem). *Open City* 9 (1999): 117–118.

Kennedy, Hunter. "Kitty Hawk" (story). *Open City* 12 (2001): 137–150.

Kharms, Daniil. "Case P-81210, Vol. 2, 1st Edition," "From Kharms's Journal," "A Humorous Division of the World in Half (Second Half)," "Blue Notebook No. 10" (poems). *Open City* 8 (1999): 130–136.

Kidd, Chip. Photographs. *Open City* 3 (1995): 129–133.

Kilimnick, Karen. "Untitled (Acid Is Groovy)" (photographs). *Open City* 9 (1999): 181–186; back cover.

Kim, Suji Kwock. "Aubade Ending with Lines from the Japanese" (poem). *Open City* 17 (2003): 117–118.

Kimball, Michael. "The Birds, the Light, Eating Breakfast, Getting Dressed, and How I Tried to Make It More of a Morning for My Wife" (story). *Open City* 20 (2005): 197–199.

Kinder, Chuck. "The Girl with No Face" (story). *Open City* 17 (2003): 31–38.

Kirby, Matthew. "The Lower Brudeckers" (story). *Open City* 22 (2006): 23–26.

Kirk, Joanna. "Clara" (drawings). *Open City* 11 (2000): 173–184.

Kleiman, Moe. "Tomorrow We Will Meet the Enemy" (poem). *Open City* 15 (2002): 119–120.

Klink, Joanna. "Lodestar" (poem). *Open City* 17 (2003): 109–110.

Knox, Jennifer L. "While Some Elegant Dancers Perched on Wires High Above a Dark, Dark Farm" (poem). *Open City* 19 (2004): 129–130.

Koestenbaum, Wayne. "First Dossier/Welcome Tour" (fiction/nonfiction). *Open City* 23 (2007): 115–124.

Koolhaas, Rem, with Harvard Project on the City. "Pearl River Delta, China" (photographs, graphs, text). *Open City* 6 (1998): 60–76.

Koons, Jeff. Photographs. *Open City* 1 (1992): 24–25.

Körmeling, John. "Drawings" (drawings). *Open City* 14 (2001–2002): 129–136.

Kotzen, Kip. "Skate Dogs" (story). *Open City* 2 (1993): 50–53.

Levine, Margaret. "In a Dream It Happens," "Dilemma" (poems). *Open City* 16 (2002–2003): 159–160.

Lewinsky, Monica. "I Am a Pizza" (poem). *Open City* 6 (1998): 129.

Lewis, Jeremy. Introduction to "Happy Deathbeds." *Open City* 4 (1996): 49–52.

Lichtenstein, Miranda. "Stills from *The Naked City*" and "Untitled, #4 (Richardson Park)" (photographs). *Open City* 12 (2001): 275–284; front and back covers.

Lichtenstein, Miranda. "Ganzfeld" (photograph). *Open City* 21 (2005–2006): front and back covers.

Lida, David. "Bewitched" (story). *Open City* 9 (1999): 69–90.

Lindbloom, Eric. "Ideas of Order at Key West" (photographs). *Open City* 6 (1998): 155–161.

Lipsyte, Sam. "Shed" (story). *Open City* 3 (1995): 226–227.

Lipsyte, Sam. "Old Soul" (story). *Open City* 7 (1999): 79–84.

Lipsyte, Sam. "Cremains" (story). *Open City* 9 (1999): 167–176.

Lipsyte, Sam. "The Special Cases Lounge" (novel excerpt). *Open City* 13 (2001): 27–40.

Lipsyte, Sam. "Nate's Pain Is Now" (story). *Open City* 22 (2006): 1–8.

Longo, Giuseppe O. "In Zenoburg" (story), trans. David Mendel. *Open City* 12 (2001): 153–160.

Longo, Giuseppe O. "Rehearsal for a Deserted City" (story), trans. Martin Fawkes. *Open City* 15 (2002): 95–103.

Longo, Giuseppe O. "Conjectures about Hell" (story), trans. James B. Michels. *Open City* 25 (2008): 183–190.

Longo, Giuseppe O. "Braised Beef for Three" (story), trans. David Mendel. *Open City* 19 (2004): 135–148.

Lopate, Phillip. "Tea at the Plaza" (essay). *Open City* 21 (2005–2006): 15–20.

Macklin, Elizabeth, trans., "The House Style," "A Qualifier of Superlatives" (poems). *Open City* 7 (1999): 107–111.

Macklin, Elizabeth, trans., "The River," "Visit" (poems) by Kirmen Uribe. *Open City* 17 (2003): 131–134.

Madoo, Ceres. "Drawings" (drawings). *Open City* 20 (2005): 149–154.

Malone, Billy. "Tanasitease" (drawings). *Open City* 21 (2005–2006): 91–96.

Malkmus, Steve. "Bennington College Rap" (poem). *Open City* 7 (1999): 46.

Mamet, David. "Boulder Purey" (poem). *Open City* 3 (1995): 187–188.

Manrique, Jaime. "Twilight at the Equator" (story). *Open City* 2 (1993): 130–134.

Marinovich, Matt. "My Public Places" (story). *Open City* 13 (2001): 67–70.

Marshall, Chan. "Fever Skies" (poem). *Open City* 9 (1999): 187.

Martin, Cameron. "Planes" (paintings). *Open City* 15 (2002): 49–57.

Mendel, David, trans., "Braised Beef for Three" (story) by Giuseppe O. Longo. *Open City* 19 (2004): 135–148.

Mengestu, Dinaw. "Home at Last" (essay). *Open City* 24 (2007–2008): 107–112.

Merlis, Jim. "One Man's Theory" (story). *Open City* 10 (2000): 171–182.

Metres, Philip and Tatiana Tulchinsky, trans., "This Is Me" (poem) by Lev Rubinshtein. *Open City* 15 (2002): 121–134.

Michels, James B., trans., "Conjectures about Hell" (story) by Giuseppe O. Longo. *Open City* 25 (2008): 183–190.

Michels, Victoria Kohn. "At the Nightingale-Bamford School for Girls" (poem). *Open City* 4 (1996): 166–167.

Middlebrook, Jason. "APL #1 Polar Bear" (drawing). *Open City* 18 (2003–2004): front and back covers.

Milford, Kate. Photographs. *Open City* 2 (1993): 54–56.

Milford, Matthew. "Civil Servants" (paintings, text). *Open City* 7 (1999): 47–55.

Miller, Greg. "Intercessor" (poem). *Open City* 11 (2000): 51.

Miller, Jane. "From *A Palace of Pearls*" (poem). *Open City* 17 (2003): 157–160.

Miller, Matt. "Driver" (poem). *Open City* 12 (2001): 169–170.

Miller, Matt. "Chimera" (poem). *Open City* 21 (2005–2006): 119–120.

Miller, Stephen Paul. "When Listening to the Eighteen-and-a-Half Minute Tape Gap as Electronic Music" (poem). *Open City* 4 (1996): 162.

M.I.M.E. Photographs. *Open City* 9 (1999): 207–218.

Mobilio, Albert. "Adhesiveness: There Was This Guy" (story). *Open City* 5 (1997): 55–56.

Moeckel, Thorpe. "Johnny Stinkbait Bears His Soul" (story). *Open City* 23 (2007): 157–162.

Moeckel, Thorpe. "Dream of My Father," "Nature Poem, Inc.," "Mussels," "At the Co-op," "Beautiful Jazz" (poems). *Open City* 23 (2007): 163–171.

Moody, Rick. "Dead Man Writes," "Domesticity," "Immortality," "Two Sonnets for Stacey" (poems). *Open City* 6 (1998): 83–88.

Moore, Honor. "She Remembers," "The Heron" (poems). *Open City* 13 (2001): 71–78.

Moore, Honor. "In Place of an Introduction" (assemblage). *Open City* 17 (2003): 105–106.

Moore, Honor. "Homage," "Hotel Brindisi," "Tango" (poems). *Open City* 20 (2005): 77–80.

Mortensen, Viggo. "From *Hole in the Sun*" (photographs). *Open City* 18 (2003–2004): 141–150.

Moss, Stanley. "Satyr Song" (memoir). *Open City* 24 (2007–2008): 137–145.

Paco. "Clown White" (story). *Open City* 3 (1995): 103–110.

Paco. "Ing," "Cross and Sundial," "Flares," (stories), "Firecrackers and Sneakers" (poem). *Open City* 9 (1999): 219–226.

Pagk, Paul. Drawings. *Open City* 5 (1997): 89–98.

Panurgias, Basile. "The Sixth Continent" (story). *Open City* 5 (1997): 81–89.

Pape, Eric. "Faces of the Past and the Future" (essay). *Open City* 22 (2006): 13–25.

Passaro, Vince. "Cathedral Parkway" (story). *Open City* 1 (1992): 26–34.

Passaro, Vince. "Adult Content" (story). *Open City* 13 (2001): 227–235.

Passaro, Vince. "Voluntary Tyranny, or Brezhnev at the Mall: Notes from Wartime on the Willful Abdication of the Liberty We Claim We're Busy Promoting Elsewhere" (essay). *Open City* 22 (2006): 39–56.

Patterson, G. E. "Drift Land" (poem). *Open City* 17 (2003): 137–138.

Pavlic, Ed. "You Sound Unseen" (poem). *Open City* 9 (1999): 227.

Pavlic, Ed. "From *Arachnida Speak*" (poem). *Open City* 16 (2002–2003): 155–157.

Pelevin, Victor. "Who By Fire" (story), trans. Matvei Yankelevich. *Open City* 7 (1999): 95–106.

Penone, Giuseppe. "Reversing One's Own Eyes" (photograph). *Open City* 9 (1999): 91–94.

Perry, Susan. "The Final Man" (story). *Open City* 8 (1999): 155–171.

Petrantoni, Lorenzo. "1880" (collages). *Open City* 21 (2005–2006): 21–28.

Phillips, Alex. "Stonemason's Oratory," "Work Shy," "Dressmaker" (poems). *Open City* 21 (2005–2006): 49–51.

Phillips, Robert. Introduction to "T. S. Eliot's Squint" by Delmore Schwartz. *Open City* 5 (1997): 152.

Pierson, Melissa Holbrook. "Night Flight" (poem). *Open City* 13 (2001): 131.

Pinchbeck, Daniel. "Fleck" (story). *Open City* 10 (2000): 239–272.

Pinchbeck, Peter. Paintings. *Open City* 13 (2001): 215–226.

Pitts-Gonzalez, Leland. "The Blue Dot" (story). *Open City* 22 (2006): 71–86.

Poirier, Mark Jude. "Happy Pills" (story). *Open City* 17 (2003): 39–50.

Polito, Robert. "The Last Rock Critic" (story). *Open City* 1 (1992): 71–78.

Polito, Robert. Introduction to "Incident in God's Country." *Open City* 4 (1996): 167–168.

Polito, Robert. "Please Refrain from Talking During the Movie" (poem). *Open City* 17 (2003): 111–112.

Poor, Maggie. "Frog Pond" (story). *Open City* 4 (1996): 163–165.

Porter, Sarah. "The Blood of Familiar Objects" (story). *Open City* 14 (2001–2002): 25–31.

Primack, Gretchen. "It Is Green" (poem). *Open City* 18 (2003–2004): 153–154.

Rothman, Richard. "Photographs" (photographs). *Open City* 6 (1998): 116–124.

Rubinshtein, Lev. "This Is Me" (poem), trans. Philip Metres and Tatiana Tulchinsky. *Open City* 15 (2002): 121–134.

Rubinstein, Raphael, trans., "From *Letter to Antonio Saura*" (story) by Marcel Cohen. *Open City* 17 (2003): 217–225.

Ruda, Ed. "The Seer" (story). *Open City* 1 (1992): 15.

Ruppersberg, Allen. "Greetings from L.A." (novel). *Open City* 16 (2002–2003): throughout.

Rush, George. "Interior, Exterior, Portrait, Still-Life, Landscape" (print). *Open City* 19 (2004): 73–83.

Ruvo, Christopher. "Afternoon, 1885" (poem). *Open City* 18 (2003–2004): 185–186.

Rux, Carl Hancock. "Geneva Cottrell, Waiting for the Dog to Die" (play). *Open City* 13 (2001): 189–213.

Salamun, Tomaz. "VI," "VII" (poems), trans. author and Joshua Beckman. *Open City* 15 (2002): 155–157.

Salvatore, Joseph. "Practice Problem" (story). *Open City* 7 (1999): 127–135.

Samore, Sam and Max Henry. "Hobo Deluxe, A Cinema of Poetry" (photographs and text). *Open City* 12 (2001): 257–270.

Samton, Matthew. "Y2K, or How I Learned to Stop Worrying and Love the CD-Rom" (poem). *Open City* 12 (2001): 191–196.

Saroyan, Strawberry. "Popcorn" (story). *Open City* 6 (1998): 125–128.

Saroyan, Strawberry. "Strawberry Is" (poem). *Open City* 26 (2008–2009): 73–80.

Sayrafiezadeh, Saïd. "My Mother and the Stranger" (story). *Open City* 17 (2003): 59–66.

Schaeffer, Doug. "Withdrawn" (collages). *Open City* 24 (2007–2008): 93–98 and back cover.

Schleinstein, Bruno. "Drawings" (drawings). *Open City* 17 (2003): 227–237.

Schles, Ken. Two untitled photographs. *Open City* 1 (1992): front and back covers.

Schles, Ken. Photography. *Open City* 2 (1993): front cover.

Schles, Ken. Two photographs. *Open City* 10 (2000): front and back covers.

Schles, Ken. "New York City: Street Photographs Following the Terrorist Attack on the World Trade Center, September 2001" (photographs). *Open City* 14 (2001–2002): 219–232.

Schmidt, Elizabeth. "Crossing Chilmark Pond," "Quiet Comfort" (poems). *Open City* 26 (2008–2009): 25–31.

Schneider, Ryan. "Mattress," "I Will Help You Destroy This, World" (poems). *Open City* 18 (2003–2004): 249–250.

Schoolwerth, Pieter. "Premonitions" (drawings). *Open City* 12 (2001): 161–168.

Schwartz, Delmore. "T. S. Eliot's Squint" (story). *Open City* 5 (1997): 152–157.

Smith, Charlie. "A Selection Process," "Agents of the Moving Company," "Evasive Action" (poems). *Open City* 6 (1998): 43–46.

Smith, Lee. Two untitled poems. *Open City* 3 (1995): 224–225.

Smith, Lee. "The Balsawood Man" (story). *Open City* 10 (2000): 203–206.

Smith, Molly. "untitled (underlie)" (drawings). *Open City* 21 (2005–2006): 41–48.

Smith, Peter Nolan. "Why I Miss Junkies" (story). *Open City* 13 (2001): 115–129.

Smith, Peter Nolan. "Better Lucky Than Good" (story). *Open City* 19 (2004): 65–70.

Smith, Rod. "Sandaled" (poem). *Open City* 14 (2001–2002): 145.

Snyder, Rick. "No Excuse," "Pop Poem '98" (poems). *Open City* 8 (1999): 151–152.

Smith, Dean. "Head Fake" (poem). *Open City* 1 (1992): 19–20.

Smith, Scott. "The Egg Man" (story). *Open City* 20 (2005): 1–67.

Solotaroff, Ivan. "Love Poem (On 53rd and 5th)" (poem). *Open City* 3 (1995): 228.

Solotaroff, Ivan. "Prince of Darkness" (story). *Open City* 6 (1998): 97–114.

Solotroff, Mark. "Fe·nes·tral Drawings" (drawings). *Open City* 18 (2003–2004): 213–218.

Southern, Nile. "Cargo of Blasted Mainframes" (story, drawings). *Open City* 1 (1992): 62–70.

Southern, Terry. "Twice on Top" (screenplay). *Open City* 2 (1993): 82–92.

Southern, Terry. "*C'est Toi Alors*: Scenario for Existing Props and French Cat" (screenplay). *Open City* 13 (2001): 41–43.

Space3. "Street Report EHV 003-2001" (prints). *Open City* 15 (2002): 159–164.

Spain, Chris. "The Least Wrong Thing" (story). *Open City* 26 (2008–2009): 33–52.

Specktor, Matthew. "A King in Mirrors" (story). *Open City* 26 (2008–2009): 59–72.

Staffel, Tim. "December 24, 1999–January 1, 2000" (story), trans. Elke Siegel and Paul Fleming. *Open City* 12 (2001): 95–118.

Stahl, Jerry. "Gordito" (story). *Open City* 22 (2006): 9–14.

Starkey, David. "Poem to Beer" (poem). *Open City* 12 (2001): 73–72.

Stefans, Brian Kim. "Two Pages from *The Screens*" (poem). *Open City* 14 (2001–2002): 163–165.

Stefans, Cindy. Photographs. *Open City* 6 (1998): 37–42.

Stefans, Cindy. Photographs. *Open City* 10 (2000): 115–124.

Stein, Lorin, trans., "Scenes from a Family Life" (story) by Véronique Ovaldé. *Open City* 21 (2005–2006): 141–152.

Stone, Nick. "Their Hearts Were Full of Spring" (photographs, text). *Open City* 10 (2000): 89–94.

Stone, Robert. "High Wire" (story). *Open City* 25 (2008): 1–38.

Strand, Mark. "Great Dog Poem No. 5" (poem). *Open City* 4 (1996): 145–146.

Stroffolino, Chris. "Nocturne," "Red Tape Sale" (poems). *Open City* 18 (2003–2004): 115–118.

Turner, Ben Carlton. "Composition Field 1," "Composition Field 2," "Soft-Core Porno" (poems). *Open City* 25: 123–130.

Uklanski, Piotr. "Queens" (photograph). *Open City* 8 (1999): front and back covers.

Uribe, Kirmen. "The River," "Visit" (poems) trans. Elizabeth Macklin. *Open City* 17 (2003): 131–134.

Vapnyar, Lara. "Mistress" (story). *Open City* 15 (2002): 135–153.

Vapnyar, Lara. "There Are Jews in My House" (story). *Open City* 17 (2003): 243–273.

Vicente, Esteban. Paintings. *Open City* 3 (1995): 75–80.

Vicuña, Cecilia. "The Brilliance of Orifices," "Mother of Pearl," "The Anatomy of Paper" (poems), trans. Rosa Alcalá. *Open City* 14 (2001–2002): 151–154.

Walker, Wendy. "Sophie in the Catacombs" (story). *Open City* 19 (2004): 131–132.

Wallace, David Foster. "Nothing Happened" (story). *Open City* 5 (1997): 63–68.

Walls, Jack. "Hi-fi" (story). *Open City* 13 (2001): 237–252.

Walser, Alissa. "Given" (story), trans. Elizabeth Gaffney. *Open City* 8 (1999): 141–150.

Walsh, J. Patrick III. "It's time to go out on your own." (drawings). *Open City* 19 (2004): 35–40.

Wareck, Sarah Borden. "The Ambassador's Daughter" (story). *Open City* 25 (2008): 107–122.

Wareham, Dean. "Swedish Fish," "Orange Peel," "Weird and Woozy," "Romantica" (song lyrics). *Open City* 15 (2002): 197–200.

Webb, Charles H. "Vic" (poem). *Open City* 4 (1996): 134.

Weber, Paolina. Two Untitled Poems. *Open City* 3 (1995): 72–74.

Weber, Paolina. "Tape" (poems). *Open City* 9 (1999): 95–106.

Wefali, Amine. "Westchester Burning" (story). *Open City* 15 (2002): 59–75

Weiner, Cynthia. "Amends" (story). *Open City* 17 (2003): 71–89.

Welsh, Irvine. "Eurotrash" (story). *Open City* 3 (1995): 165–186.

Welsh, Irvine. "The Rosewell Incident" (story). *Open City* 5 (1997): 103–114.

Wenderoth, Joe. "Where God Is Glad" (essay). *Open City* 23 (2007): 209–216.

Wenderoth, Joe. "College," "Wedding Vow," "Against Zoning" (poems). *Open City* 23: (2007): 217–219.

Wenthe, William. "Against Witness" (poem). *Open City* 6 (1998): 115.

Wenthe, William. "Against Witness" (poem). *Open City* 12 (2001): 273.

Wenthe, William. "Shopping in Artesia" (poem). *Open City* 19 (2004): 63.

Wetzsteon, Rachel. "Largo," "Gusts" (poems). *Open City* 12 (2001): 285–286.

Weyland, Jocko. "Burrito" (story). *Open City* 6 (1998): 27–36.

Weyland, Jocko. "Swimmer Without a Cause" (story). *Open City* 10 (2000): 231–238.

Weyland, Jocko. "The Elk and the Skateboarder" (story). *Open City* 15 (2002): 169–187.